ATLANTIC COUNTY GHOST STORIES

by

CHARLES J. ADAMS III

EXETER HOUSE BOOKS

ATLANTIC COUNTY
GHOST STORIES
by Charles J. Adams III

©2003

Exeter House Books
P.O. Box 6411
Wyomissing, PA 19610
www.exeterhousebooks.com

ISBN 978-1-880683-17-0

2009 Edition
First Edition June 2003
Printed in the United States of America

All photographs by the author, except for back cover, lower
right photo, courtesy of Atlantic City Convention & Visitors Authority
All post cards from the collection of the author.

ON THE COVER: The Atlantic County Courthouse in Mays Landing

This book is dedicated to the ghost of the Shoreham Hotel, where my
parents and I enjoyed many good times many years ago.

Table of Contents

Introduction

S omething quite curious happened on the way to the completion of this book.

Although, as indicated by its title, this volume is a collection of ghost stories and legends of Atlantic *County*, you will notice a dearth of tales from its largest municipality, Atlantic *City*.

It is not for lack of trying to track down accounts of haunted places there. From Ducktown to the Inlet, the Boardwalk to the bay, the lighthouse to the library, we read, researched, knocked on doors, phoned, and emailed but came up with very little.

We spoke with just about everybody who's anybody in Atlantic City historical circles and discovered that they agree there is a paucity of the paranormal in "America's Playground."

That could well be that the city has been too busy playing to take account of its haunted heritage.

Robert Ruffolo, the keeper of a treasure chest of local art and artifacts at his Princeton Antiques & Books shop on Atlantic Ave., did his level best to stir up some stories. He placed calls on our behalf to Atlantic City old-timers and *cognoscente*, but came up with nothing.

Acclaimed authority of local lore "Boo" Pergament searched the memory bank of his mind and recalled no ghost stories. Ditto for author and Atlantic City *grande dame* Vicki Gold Levi, who recalled a wealth of anecdotes but no ghost stories.

GHOST STORIES OF ATLANTIC COUNTY

Prolific ghost story writer Jo Kapus also rummaged through her files, contacts, and memory and came up dry.

The Absecon Lighthouse and keeper's house, which *look* and *should be* haunted–are not, according to its staff. Likewise from the folks at the Atlantic City Convention & Visitors Authority offices in Boardwalk Hall. If any place in Atlantic City might harbor ghosts, or at least stories of the unexplained, it would be that storied building. But, it does not.

And the casinos? We reached very high levels at most of them but were rebuffed when the thought that there may be ghosts gliding amidst the guests.

In a fit of whimsy (very well, desperation), we even did a web search: "Atlantic City+ghosts+haunted." Within seconds, the results yielded a site that gave momentary hope.

But alas, the "Atlantic City" was in Wyoming and the "+ghosts" were metaphors. Atlantic City, Wyoming is a Wild West boomtown gone bust.

Atlantic City, New Jersey, is a busttown gone boom. However, it seems that the coming of that *boom* resulted in the passing of the *boo!* from the storied resorts legend ledger.

Is Atlantic City haunted? Of course it is.

Everyone who remembers A.C./B.C. (Atlantic City Before Casinos) has their own cast of phantoms: The Diving Horse, Tony Grant's Stars of Tomorrow, Mr. Peanut, Grady & Hurst, Captain Starn–and on, and on.

The footprint of modern Atlantic City trod heavily and heartlessly on the sandy soil of the northern end of Absecon Island. The massive money machines that set up shop may have forever changed the look of the city but cannot totally destroy the legacy of those who built the city and the spirits of those who hold its history dear to their hearts.

One of those individuals is John Polillo, whose passion plays out in the images he and his twin brother have preserved. At "PostCardShow.com," the Polillo brothers deal in and display cards–not the kind of cards dealt on the gaming tables, but the kind of post cards that flooded the Atlantic City Post Office in the early 20th century.

But what about ghosts? "I don't believe in ghosts," John Polillo said as we sat at the reception desk of the Atlantic City Historical Museum. He and others there agreed that folks in Atlantic City have never put too much stock in ghost stories.

They indicated that the political and economic climate of Atlantic City during the casino-building years wiped out much of not only the physical "old" but also the spiritual feeling of and for the city.

Some blamed political indifference and incompetence for the lack of historical preservation in the city. Only a handful of historic sites remain after the city reinvented itself in the 1970s, and only a handful of citizens seem to care enough to ensure that what remains will be retained.

In some senses, Atlantic City is a small town masquerading as a world-class resort. Sadly, however, the small town within that city seems at times to be shrinking to oblivion.

But what was so curious about our quixotic quest for ghost stories in Atlantic City is that nowhere did

anyone wink their eye and fabricate a fable just to read
their name, or their business' name, in a book. It has
been attempted, detected, and rejected in past research
missions.

That tells me something. That tells me that ghosts
of convenience, phantoms of financial gain, or specters
of special interests did not rise to attempt to haunt
these pages.

Atlantic City is haunted by more than just the
allegorical apparitions of days gone by. Ghosts do
gather in the tattered corridors of timeworn old
buildings, on properties now consumed by modern
buildings, and, yes, in the glittering casino hotels.

Spirits stroll the Boardwalk, the gaming floors, and
even in the parking garages of Atlantic City—of that
there is no doubt.

At certain times and in certain places during the
research phase of this book, members of our research
team detected untoward energies in some of those
places. For ethical and legal reasons, however, those
contacts were not detailed in this volume because the
property owners either could not be located or would
not approve publication of a ghost story related to their
establishment. Although somewhat miffed by that
attitude, we fully understand and respect it.

But, there is always a "Book Two!" If you are in
touch, please be in touch.

Charles J. Adams III
June, 2003

Greg Gregory at the top of a staircase where spirits dwell at Gregory's Restaurant in Somers Point

Are You There, Uncle Eddie?

Nothing is as it seems in the historic building that houses Gregory's, a landmark restaurant in the heart of Somers Point.

Its architectural anomalies and ribald history can be explained.

GHOST STORIES OF ATLANTIC COUNTY

What lurks within its dark corridors, steep staircases, and mysterious chambers far from the dining rooms is another story—a *ghost* story

"Who knows," said waitress Kathy Kearney. "There could be energies coming from each and every board in this place!"

Interesting proposition, indeed. But, what did Ms. Kearney mean by her statement?

Should you wander through the innards of the building at Delaware Avenue and Shore Road, you will find that doors are of varying sizes, boards and lumber never seem to match, and although the place is solid and substantial, certain areas seem somehow out of kilter.

That's because when it was built in 1908, the structure was pieced together mainly from wood salvaged from homes that were flattened by a severe storm that ravaged Longport. The wood was barged across the bay to Somers Point and used to build what began as a private residence and dry goods store.

Gerald S. Piercy opened a self-named hotel there in 1913, and through to 1946 it continued as a bar, hotel, and—you will read the rest.

"When my grandmother bought the place," Gregory Gregory, the current owner said, "she asked the previous owner where he makes the most of the money." Of course, the innocent question was to provide a guideline for the new owner as to what was the biggest attraction and thus the biggest revenue source. Would it be the food, the drinks?

It turned out that it was the 15 rooms upstairs. Their value as hotel rooms was minimal. Their value as the, shall we say, "hospitality suites" for 15 "working girls" was inestimable. The "kickback" from those girls to the innkeeper was a steady source of income.

Today, what went on in those second floor boudoirs is part and parcel to a steady source of eerie activities in the old hotel.

"We've had numerous waitresses and cooks spot one of the ladies over the years," Gregory said, noting that the ghosts of the "women of the night" are quite commonly felt, heard, and seen there. Unexplainable sounds of all sorts have come from those dark chambers, now used only for storage. Footsteps, thumps and bumps, and, yes, the creaking of bedsprings and heavy breathing have echoed inside the rooms where "pleasures" were once taken.

It is difficult to walk through those rooms and down the corridor that connects them without feeling the sensation that much human drama has played out there. The energies that swirl inside those walls are palpable.

When the Gregory family purchased the building in 1946, they aimed to upgrade and improve its image. Several improvements and modifications were made over the years, but the historical integrity of the building has been maintained as much as possible.

In the basement, wall paintings behind shelving units are reminders of the years that the subterranean room was a Prohibition-era speakeasy.

Upstairs, the old bawdyhouse rooms are used for offices and storage. During the earlier years of the Gregory family's ownership, they were used to house men who helped to build the Ocean City Bridge and then men who simply needed a cheap place to live.

And die.

Gregory's Restaurant, Somers Point

"When I was a kid," Gregory said, "and I'll never forget this, I used to hang around here with my pop. He had a little round mirror near the cash register. One time I asked him what it was for. He said, oh, we use that in the upstairs rooms to see if the guys are breathing.

"One time, one of the old guys hadn't been downstairs for several days. My pop told me to go check on him. He gave me a passkey and the mirror. I looked at him and I swore he was dead. I put the mirror up in front of his nose for a split second and pulled away. I was scared!

4

"I went down and whispered to my father that the man was dead. My dad went back up with me and held the mirror to his nose. He laughed and yelled out to me, 'he's not dead! He's drunk!!'"

That chap may not have died in one of the rooms, but others have. And, their restless spirits remain there. The door of into an empty room directly across the hall from Greg's upstairs office often opens on its own, despite it being securely latched shut only moments before. Greg has had numerous reports from employees who have seen shadowy figures cavorting in the rooms–lights that switch on and off, silhouettes that skulk down the hall; the occasional disembodied moan and groan.

One ghost that Greg Gregory and his sister, Darcy, have identified is "Uncle Eddie." "He was a cleanup man," Greg recalled. "He was my grandmother's brother."

As somewhat of a "family ghost," Eddie is thought of fondly at Gregory's. However, that does not prevent everyone–even family–from being a bit put off by his presence.

"He's the guy people see in the kitchen from time to time," Greg said of Eddie's ghost. "They'll see an old, white-haired guy in the kitchen. He used to make the soups there. We've had some people come in and actually strike up a conversation with him before he vanishes."

The ghost has been seen wearing a brown satin "Gregory's" jacket with "Uncle Eddie" embroidered on the front. It was his pride and joy, said Greg. "He would wear that if it was 200 degrees below zero!"

5

Eddie also had a very recognizable laugh. "When some people say they had conversations with the white-haired man in the kitchen," Greg continued, "I'd ask them if they heard him laugh. They said yes, and when they imitated the ghost's laugh, I recognized it right away as Eddie's."

Interestingly, Eddie did not pass away inside Gregory's.

"He didn't die here," Greg Gregory asserted, "but he lost his soul here."

There are other peculiar ghosts at Gregory's. The old rathskeller harbors a few.

"Some of our people will go down to the basement," Darcy Gregory said, "and they'll come running upstairs and tell us they're never going down there again.

They say they feel a cold breeze go by them and feel as if someone was lurking just over their shoulders."

Some say they have actually caught fleeting glimpses of phantoms glide in front of them.

"That's when they come running upstairs. They tell me they definitely feel a presence of someone or something and they get chills all over their bodies," Darcy added.

Most of the ghosts of Gregory's dwell in places the public will likely never venture into.

But one may manifest in full view of anyone enjoying a meal in the main dining room.

"One guy has been seen at least twice in the dining room," Greg noted. "He sits at one of the tables. He's wearing a blue pea coat.

"He sits facing north, parallel to Shore Road, at the window seat. He calls the waitress and asks for something for his snapper soup.

"Now, the old customers were notorious for drinking the sherry that came with the soup. They'd drink anything. When the waitress turns around and asks if he wants anything else, he's gone!"

Greg said that one employee was so shaken by the disappearing diner that she quit her job there.

Gregory's is a true Somers Point landmark. On one side of the building is a lively bar. On the other is a lovely dining area. Above them and below them are the lairs of the building's many ghosts.

The Gregory family has done much remodeling and renovating to the sturdy, albeit quirky old building over the years. That, too, may have contributed to the restlessness of its ghosts.

"Who knows," Greg mused, "maybe we shook something loose!"

☠

The "Dime Ghost" of Linwood

People have often joked they wouldn't mind having a ghost in their house if it helped do the housework every once in a while.

In a certain home on Shore Road in Linwood, the ghost or ghosts have gone one better–they have been leaving cold, hard, cash for at least two generations of owners to find.

It's not a princely sum, and it has accumulated a dime at a time. But, how those dimes get to where they have been found has confounded the current and immediate past occupants of the classic Victorian dwelling.

James Ireland, a noted sea captain, built the house in 1860. Jim Mahoney, manager of the Anchorage Tavern in Somers Point, provided the first reports of its odd haunting.

"We bought the house in 1988," Mahoney said, "and in the first couple of days we were there, I saw the vision of a woman in a purple dress."

The image, he noted, would materialize for only a few seconds and vanish as abruptly as it appeared.

"Two days after that," Mahoney continued, "I saw a person walking by our back yard. That one, too, just disappeared completely."

In those first days and weeks Mahoney and his companion took up residence in the house, visitors would also report sensing and seeing presences within its walls.

"Later," Mahoney said, "we found out that a girl had died in the well there, and her body was down there for three months before they found her."

He and his girlfriend summoned the counsel of a respected psychic who came to their home and confirmed that it was haunted by the spirit of that young girl and, possibly, several other ghosts.

"They're here," the woman told Mahoney, "and they're not really happy with you!"

This was not the response Mahoney had hoped to hear. When he asked the reader why the spirits were uneasy, she told him it was because Jim and his friend were not married and the spirits were locked into a code of Victorian morality.

Perhaps even more interesting was the historical fact that the house was built by Capt. Ireland as a wedding present to his new bride.

Undaunted by that assertion, the couple continued to make the home their own.

"The ghosts won't show themselves often," the psychic advised, "but you will find things missing from time to time."

They never dreamed that they would also find things that seemed to have no logical origin. To be specific, dimes.

"One time," Mahoney recalled, "we were doing some work and we found a perfect, absolutely perfect dime, dated 1860!"

That discovery was but the first of many that would yield both cents and sensations.

9

Jim Mahoney considers himself rather neat and fastidious. Despite his best efforts to be organized and tidy, items would often disappear and, as the psychic predicted, show up a few days later in a least likely place.

"We had a wallpaper guy do the whole house," he said. "One time, they were up on the third floor. He had a brush up there, but it disappeared. They looked around everywhere, but couldn't find it. They went out and got another brush and 15 minutes later the first brush showed up exactly where he had left it."

Jim and his mate never felt threatened by the spirit activity in the home they occupied. That was not true, however, of one of the cleaning ladies who were once employed there.

"One of them was vacuum cleaning one of the parlors," Jim said, "when she stopped. She said she couldn't move any farther. She thought someone was playing games with her.

"She turned around and there was nobody there, but she was frozen in that spot. She got goosebumps, eventually was able to run out and told everyone she would never work in that room alone again."

Jim also noticed on several occasions that his dog would often stop its frolicking, cock its head, and sniff at an unseen entity.

Jim lived in the house for only a few years and sold the property to Marietta and Frank Fattori in the early 1990s.

Marietta Fattori described the place as her "dream house," and she and her husband have made considerable renovations to the home since they moved in.

It has been during their residency that the "dime ghost" has been most active.

"The day we moved in," Marietta said, "we had several people working here with us."

As she went about her tasks, something strange happened–and happened again and again. Marietta said nothing to no one. Then, during a break in the work, one of her friends asked Marietta if she had found anything unusual as they were moving items into the house. At that point, she revealed that yes, she had found dimes–six or seven of them.

"So did I," said the incredulous friend.

"We both wondered where they came from," said a bewildered Marietta.

When she met with her husband at the home they were moving out of, she did not tip her hand but asked him if he had found anything strange while he was moving and working in their new home.

He, too, had found several dimes.

Marietta told the tale to her hairdresser, who was intrigued by the dime-dispensing ghost. He added another element of mystery to the mix by suggesting to Marietta that the dimes may be tokens, symbols that a fortune may be stashed somewhere in the house. Or, they could be omens of something to be concerned about.

Marietta dismissed any ominous meanings. "I told him no, it's not exactly writing in blood 'GET OUT!'"

Still, she wondered how and why the coins were appearing. All rational explanations were exhausted, and she and her husband had dismissed any notions of pranks being played by their friends.

"It really did get to my husband," Marietta said. "It spooked him."

The reading of a psychic and the support of their friends soothed any apprehensions the couple may have had.

"It was a happy spirit, I was told, and I didn't think much more about it," said Marietta. "I don't think it's anything negative. We seem to find them whenever we're doing something in the house. We don't know when, and we don't know where they'll turn up."

Frank Fattori agreed. "The strangest one I ever had was down at my work bench. I spotted a dime. I remember it was 'heads-up.' I went away to do something else for a few minutes and when I came back, the dime was 'tails-up!'"

Frank said he really isn't frightened by all of it, just miffed. "I'd say there have been 60 to 70 dimes found around the house. I've found 25 or 30 myself."

Pam Johnston is a friend of Marietta's and is as confused as anyone about the phenomena.

"They'd be just anywhere," she said. "On the third floor, on the landing coming down the stairs. Sometimes they'd be right out where you could see them and many times, they'd be just tucked out of the way. Sometimes you'd have to look twice, and there it was, another dime.

"It was scary," she added, "Those dimes were everywhere!"

The ghost–or whatever it is–continues to drop the dimes in the Fattori residence. In fact, shortly before

Marietta and Frank were interviewed for this story, they found another one!

Pam Johnston watches the house when the Fattoris are away. "I would think there was someone in the house with me," she said. "But I knew there wasn't." Furthermore, she is convinced the matter of the money is not a trick and is beyond any mortal's control.

"I attribute it to something supernatural," she offered. "Maybe it has something to do with other people before—and are still here."

☠

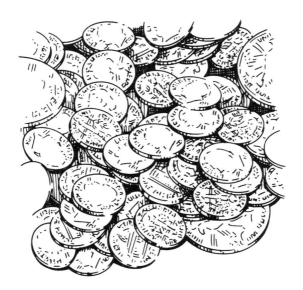

Louis Renault

The Spirit of the Cellars

I t is a bit of the Old Country in New Jersey. It is grapevines in the pines. It is one of Atlantic County's most alluring attractions.

It is the Renault Winery—and it is haunted.

Haunted, some say, by the very man who brought his vintner's skills to the heart of South Jersey in 1864.

He was Louis Nicholas Renault, who came to this country from France and found the climate and soil of the county to be very similar to that of his native area. In 1870, he brought his *New Jersey Champagne* to

14

market and soon became the nation's largest champagne distributor.

His legacy, the Renault Winery in Galloway Township, is a registered state historic site and the home of a complex that includes a gourmet restaurant, luxury hotel, golf course, and a wine and champagne glass museum.

What most visitors may never see, but may well sense, is the very spirit of Louis Renault following them as they tour the winery or taste the fruits of its vines.

Absecon native Richard Higgins has been leading tours of the winery for many years. He knows the long corridors, dark cellars, and elegant rooms with an intimacy few others possess.

And, he steadfastly rejects the notion of ghosts–at least he tries to.

"There have been many unexplainable events," Higgins admitted. "Especially in the evening, when people come to lock up, they will hear noises, footsteps, and even the sound of someone running down the hallway."

Lights may turn themselves on or off, disembodied voices may be heard–but Higgins is cautious about proclaiming his dear winery as being haunted–at least he tries to be.

"I must say," he added, "it's hard to convince myself sometimes, especially at night when I'm back here."

"Back here" is in the gloomy, roomy chamber known as the Aging Cellar. Dominated by massive, sturdy oak and redwood casks that hold anywhere from 2,000 to 4,000 gallons of wine and champagne, the cellar's pungent but pleasant odor is the very essence of a winery's appeal.

It is also a quiet, almost foreboding place that would seem ripe for the ramblings of a wraith or two.

"Oh, definitely," Higgins said. "We hear all kinds of noises down here. Usually it's a *clanking* noise, as if someone is using some kind of a wrench and drops it on occasion, things like that."

Could that person be Louis Renault, still lovingly tending his precious product?

Richard Higgins, the eternal skeptic, cannot rule out that possibility. "I've had several people on the evening tours tell me that they have felt a presence–and they always feel that it's Mr. Renault–still here," he conceded.

That Louis Renault's spirit would choose to remain at the winery would not be surprising. He is buried beneath a pink granite marker in the quiet confines of the Egg Harbor City Cemetery a few miles away. But, it was at his beloved winery where his "imprint" may well have been made.

The ghost of Renault, restless but harmless, may remain simply to oversee the wine production. Or, it may emerge whenever tour groups or special events "stir up" the solitude there. Perhaps his energies have been released because of the many renovations and additions that have been done to his old *vignoble*.

Joseph P. Milza is the head of the family that has owned the Renault Winery since 1976. At his office at the spectacular Tuscany House Hotel across the road from the winery, Milza also tried his best to minimize the thought of ghosts strolling through the old winery.

He, too, has some difficulty doing so.

"I must admit," he said, "we have seen some weird things. Many people who work here or just visit or take tours do claim that they have heard strange noises and have actually seen something."

What that "something" might be has never been fully identified. One report from an employee mentioned the fleeting glimpse of an elderly, bearded man who peeked around the corner in a hallway and disappeared. The description would fit Louis Renault's appearance.

"It's kind of weird in there at some places and at some times," Milza said of the winery. "Everybody seems to believe that Mr. Renault's spirit is in there. It's a common thing for any one of us to walk through and think or even say, 'Louie's walking through here with us.'"

Perhaps, Mr. Higgins, and perhaps, Mr. Milza, he really is.

☠

Dock's Oyster House, Atlantic City

The Protector

Dock's Oyster House has seen it all. The good times, the bad times; the good guys, the bad guys.

And, some folks believe, one of the good guys still looks over the venerable Atlantic City eatery with a protective, if not sometimes provocative eye.

He would be the late Joe Dougherty, the third generation of the Dougherty family that has owned the popular seafood restaurant since it was opened in 1897 by the first generation of the family.

They were good times back then. Atlantic City was growing into a world-class seaside resort and Harry "Dock" Dougherty took full advantage of the growing tourism trade and access to fresh seafood and opened his little oyster house.

Generation two, in the form of Harry's son, Joe, took over in 1938 and generation three, Joe Jr., assumed command in 1969.

As good as things were in the 1890s, they were that bad in the late 1960s. Atlantic City was a shell of its former glory. But Joe Jr. believed things would turn around.

He believed so strongly that he ignored the prophets of doom, doubled the size of the dining room, renovated the kitchens and dining room, bought a liquor license, and hopped on the saddle of hope to ride out the city's lean years.

His tenacity and vision—and the Dougherty family's hard work—paid dividends that have been passed on to a fourth generation, Joe III and Frank Dougherty.

Through its long and colorful history, Dock's has remained a place to see and be seen in Atlantic City.

The brightest of the Boardwalk's stars and the darkest of the old Georgia Avenue underworld scene have dined there.

It is the *otherworldly* activity there that teases the fourth generation of the family, particularly Frank Dougherty.

"I have heard my mother say that she feels that my late father is still watching over the place," Frank said.

Accordingly, whenever a light switches itself on or off, as they have been known to do; or whenever a cool breeze passes by, everyone at Dock's seems certain it is the protective spirit of Joseph R. Dougherty, Jr.

One waitress told Frank that she has heard Joe's voice on several occasions. "He used to work the line," Frank said, "he was one of the chefs. He would call out when orders were ready. She said she still hears him call her name at times."

"We've had one server who has been here for 35 years—before my father was even here—who has the same feelings at times. She thinks that he's still here, watching over everybody."

There have been reports of other ghostly images at Dock's Oyster House. "I've had at least two people who came in and told me they saw a couple sitting at the bar," Frank added. The phantom diners are seen only briefly before they vanish. "I can't trace that back to anything," Frank admitted. I don't know who they may be."

But he can trace the overpowering sensation that his father's energies remain there. He traces it to Joe Jr.'s dedication to his restaurant and love for his family. "He was always the guy who closed at night, always the last one in the place."

The Shaler Grave on Indian Cabin Road

Sibbell's Restless Spirit

S ituated in an eerily quiet setting reminiscent of the legendary Sleepy Hollow of "Headless Horseman" fame is the final resting place of Sibbell Shaler. But, the poor woman apparently gets little rest in the afterlife.

Thorny vines wrap around a bare cedar tree next to the grave. Mushrooms pop from the leaf-encrusted

21

soil. Nearby are mysterious concrete bunkers, said to have been pigpens.

In autumn, mosses coat the trees in an almost luminescent green. It is a kaleidoscope of color, but all around, everywhere, are the thorns. They are tangled hither and yon as if warning people to stay away, guarding the grave.

The thickets just beyond the weathered tombstone, restored and re-framed by preservationists in the 1960s, seem to invite the entities said to dwell there–the entities of Sibbel and, they say, her fourth child.

Can you hear the laughter? The giggling, or perhaps the sorrowful moans that echo softly in the woods? Many say they have. Many say the gravesite on Indian Cabin Road is the epicenter of a very powerful haunting.

There seems to be a thin but credible historical baseline. Sibbel was the wife of Timothy Shaler, the master of the galley "Alligator," which sailed out of Chestnut Neck in the 1780s.

Shaler was a privateer and his wife would remain at home caring for their three children while he was raiding ships off the coast of Brigantine Island.

That home stood just beyond the gravesite, but nothing is left of it.

What is left of the Shaler family are those sounds, those sights, and those sensations that have made the Shaler grave one of Atlantic County's most notorious haunted spots.

For generations, those who dare to approach the grave have been accosted by eerie sensations. The fleeting glimpse of a young woman may flit across a field. A dull glow may hover over the grave at night. Whispering and sobbing sounds seem to seep from the soil itself and send terrified voyeurs fleeing in fear.

Exactly what happened and what happens there is fraught with mystery, myth, and misunderstanding. Did Indians massacre poor Sibbell and her children? Did a horrid disease claim her and her offspring? Were they all incinerated in a fire that destroyed their house? Or, did Sibbell die in deep despair after her beloved boys were killed during the Revolutionary War?

William McCullough of Pomona, an Atlantic County native, grew up with the story that Timothy Shaler was deep in the pines hunting. "And," McCullough recalled, "while he was gone, Indians came and killed his wife and children.

"From what I understand, he was out hunting Indians. That's the last they heard from him." But, McCullough added, Shaler is alleged to have left a trail of many dead Indians as his legacy.

McCullough has heard every version of the Shaler Grave ghost story. He was once the superintendent of the Egg Harbor City Lake and Campground, and it is on that facility's grounds that the grave is located.

At the Egg Harbor City Historical Society, Ronald Hessy remembered the version of the story he heard in his youth. "There was talk that the Indians killed the family," he said, "but from what I understand her husband was a privateer." Hessy discounted the notions that disease–the plague has been mentioned–killed the Shalers and, citing the lack of any corroborative historical information, totally rejected the Indian massacre/Indian fighter tale.

The Shaler grave has spawned many stories that have been nourished by campfire storytellers and internet exchanges. What really happened to Sibbell, her husband, and her children has been lost in the fog of history.

If the inscription on the tombstone is to be believed, Sibbell, who died at age 34, is buried there with "three of her infant children."

That would discount the story that four of her sons were killed in the Revolution, the bodies of only three of them were recovered, and Sibbell's ghost wanders eternally in search of her fourth son's remains.

The tombstone's vague "*three of her...*" reference does invite speculation that there may have been more than three Shaler children, and the others were not buried with her in the family plot. That, in turn, has led to what seems to be the most recurring reason for Sibbell's restless, ever-searching soul.

Sarah

Bob Schoelkopf is a practical kind of guy who is not prone to flights of fear or fancy.

He and his wife, Sheila Dean, have dedicated their lives to the rescue, rehabilitation, and release of stranded or distressed marine mammals and sea turtles that wash ashore along the New Jersey coast.

In 1978, they founded the Marine Mammal Stranding Center, which with its Sea Life Educational Center has become a popular attraction as well as a vital service to creatures of the sea.

Alas, there seems to be no spectral activity at the Brigantine center, but this is not to say that Bob and Sheila haven't had their shares of encounters with the unknown.

In the mid-1990s, the couple purchased a house in Galloway Township. It wasn't long until they realized that they were not alone there.

"After settlement," Bob said, "we had noticed that all the power had been turned off instead of it being turned on for us."

So, they did the best they could with lanterns and flashlights their first night in their new residence.

"Our neighbors saw flashlights in the house, so my wife went across the street to let them know that it was us, not prowlers," he added.

Bob continued his story. "The only piece of furniture we had was a big rocker at the bottom of the stairs.

"Also in the room was a potbelly stove. So, I decided that without the electricity we could warm it up a little by building a fire. We had the fire going and I was sitting in the rocker while my wife was across the street.

"I looked up the stairs and I saw a face–a woman's face looking from the top of the railing down at me. Well, I thought it was just the light from the fire playing tricks."

He would learn within minutes that it was not an illusion.

"My wife came from across the street and she told me she had talked to the neighbors and, guess what? We have a ghost in our new house, she told me."

Upstaging his wife, Bob offered with a coy confidence, "Yeah, and it's a female, right?"

His wife was incredulous. "How do you know that," she asked.

"Because I just met her," Bob replied.

That quickly, it was established by an outside source and by Bob's observation that their house was, like it or not, haunted.

By whom remains a mystery.

"Well," Bob said, "we named her Sarah, because out back in the shack, when we opened the door it said 'Sarah.' Someone had written the name on the back of the door."

As it turned out, they learned that Sarah was a previous resident of the house, but not likely its *permanent* resident. The identity of that spirit is still unknown.

"We did find out that a young girl had died in the house many years ago," Bob said, "and the people before us who had the house were so superstitious that they had people come in to try to cleanse the house. They were very nervous about it, and when I brought it up to the woman who had previously owned the house, she got white as a ghost herself. She didn't want anybody to know that the place was haunted, because she felt they may have not been able to sell it."

That previous resident was so spooked that she placed arrowheads on every windowsill in an attempt to ward off the ghosts. She reportedly also had several exorcists attempt, apparently unsuccessfully, to purge the place of its entities.

Bob and Sheila accepted their usually invisible housemate as a benign being whose countenance could be called upon to provide some entertainment for certain visitors.

One evening, several members of the board of directors of the Stranding Center were there. "We had told one of them about Sarah," Bob said, "and he laughed it off. He said that anyone who believed in ghosts is crazy."

Moments later, that skeptic almost ate his words—literally. "After the meeting, he was in the middle of the room. There's a mirror on the wall that has a hat rack on it, and there was a wicker basket hanging from it. He was about five feet away from it when the basket just left the mirror, flew straight across the room some five feet, and hit him on the head," Bob said.

"He thought we had pulled a prank, but we were all standing far from the basket, and trust me, we did not."

Did the incident change that chap's mind about the existence of ghosts? "Well," Bob chuckled, "he doesn't want to come to our house for meetings anymore!"

Although they are relatively comfortable with the ghost of "Sarah," or whomever, Bob and Sheila have tried to quiet it.

Sheila had been on a boat in the Bahamas in October, 1999, and there were many healers and psychics aboard. "I related our stories to one of them," she said, "and she told me I should go back and tell the spirit that it was OK to leave, that it didn't have to stay there anymore.

"I did just that. I said it aloud. I said 'Sarah, you may leave now. We'll take good care of your house for you.' And after that, we didn't have any incidents like we did in the beginning."

☠

A ghost reportedly walks within the walls of the Daniel Estell House at Estell Manor Park.

Ghosts of a Ghost Town

Look at a detailed map of Atlantic County, New Jersey, and you will see them. Scattered between towns such as Hammonton, Mays Landing, and Egg Harbor City are broad grids of streets that mark the existence of other places–that do not exist.

The notion of ghost towns conjures up images of the boom/bust mining towns of the west. But, Atlantic County has more than its share of them.

They have names like Laureldale, Thelma, Finger Boards, and Gigantic City.

GHOST STORIES OF ATLANTIC COUNTY

Many are so ghostly that they exist only on paper and in the fading imaginations of failed entrepreneurs. Some were the dreams of developers who hoped for a windfall of building along the highways and railroads that coursed the county on their ways from cities to shores. Others were classic "company towns" built to house and serve hundreds–sometimes thousands–of workers at mills, mines, and munitions plants.

At some places, the geographical ghosts manifest as gravel lanes with grandiose labels on weathered street signs. It is not unusual to see a "15th St." or "Broadway" leading into the thick of a pine forest along routes 40, 50, or other main roads of the county.

Those dead dreamtowns usually emerged from the drawing boards as serene residential communities. But, some were the products of war.

Follow Route 50 about four miles south of Mays Landing and you will find Belcoville. Or, perhaps you will not. Should you not drive past what is left of it, you will discover what remains of the once-thriving town.

What you will not find are the stores, the bowling alley, the school, town hall, and enough houses to accommodate nearly 5,000 residents. Those are all gone now.

Nearby, you *will* find a most peculiar park called Estell Manor. Within its bounds is a broad sampling a South Jersey ghost town has to offer.

Including, of course, a ghost or two.

Wedged between the South River and the state highway are the requisite roadways of any respectable ghost town. They are populated only by squirrels, beavers, and birds. They are marked now as hiking and biking trails.

Occasionally, concrete foundations, a rail bed, or stone or brick ruins rise as silent witnesses to what Estell Manor once was.

Once, a rail line, factories, administration buildings, cafeterias, barracks, and more than 1,100 soldiers occupied the sandy land. It was the Bethlehem Loading Company complex, built in 1918 to manufacture shells for the U.S. military as it entered World War I.

Down the road a bit, the town of Belcoville (named after the *Be*thlehem *L*oading *Co*mpany) was built to supply and support plant workers.

The endeavor survived only several months, as the war ended in November, 1918. In the early 1940s, during another war, the usable steel and iron of the Loading Company was spirited away and the specters of prosperity took up residence.

The 1,700-acre park is named Estell Manor after the Estell family that once owned the land and an even earlier manufacturing facility, the Estellville Glassworks.

In dramatic ruins and on detailed placards, the story of the glassworks is detailed in a more developed area of the park.

The main glasshouse, a pot house, a flattening house, and 13 workers' homes made up the grounds, where window glass was produced from 1825 to 1877. The entire park grounds were once clear-cut to accommodate the buildings. It has all gone back to nature.

31

In keeping with that, a central feature of the park is the Warren E. Fox Nature Center. It houses the park headquarters, environmental displays, and live animal displays. It is also the location for maps and brochures, restroom facilities, and environmental information. Orienteering maps and compass courses are also available there.

It was in the nature center where John Hansen, the senior naturalist of the park, told of the hauntings of old Estellville and Estell Manor.

Yes, his focus and expertise is generally confined to the natural attributes of the area, but the *supernatural* activities that have been reported there cannot escape his attention or interest.

"Over the years talking with the various people who have lived in the area awhile and with campers who come here," he said, "and even with people who have worked here, I have been told of three ghost stories and, of course, the Jersey Devil."

Ah, the Jersey Devil. Although this legendary beast will be covered in more detail in another chapter of this book, it is worth noting that some believe that Estellville is the very "birthplace" of the creature. But, back to the ghosts of the ghost town.

"The first place would be the farmhouse right across the street from the Nature Center," Hansen noted as he motioned toward the Aaron Shaw House, a simple frame home built in 1824.

"On the second floor, people have, over the years and usually at night, seen someone looking out the window. And, of course, there would be no one in the house," Hansen said.

"It was a common thing among the park rangers for years for them to go in, check the place, turn off all the lights upstairs, go out and get back into their vehicles. They would look back and see lights on the second floor. Then, they would see someone looking out the window."

The Aaron Shaw House

They saw a silhouette with no discernible features, but they were positive every light in the house had been turned on and there was nothing near any window that could have created the appearance or illusion of someone peering out of it.

The rangers would even re-enter the building and double-check, only to find that the lights were off and nobody was in the place.

Nobody *alive*, that is.

The second haunted house at Estell Manor would appear to be just outside the park along Route 50, but is actually within the bounds.

"Over at the Daniel Estell House, which we refer to as 'the mansion,'" John Hansen said, "people have also reported ghostly sightings.

"Apparently Daniel's wife, Rebecca, walks on the third floor of that place. She died at an early age."

Noted on park maps as the "Manor House," the Daniel Estell mansion looks the part of a "haunted house."

Under reconstruction at the time of this writing, the building had been used for several years as a juvenile center.

"The kids there swore by it," Hansen said. "They continually said they heard footsteps and had seen Rebecca's ghost on the third floor."

The third spirit that has been reported in Estell Manor Park lingers at the end of Artesian Well Road, one of the so-called "corduroy roads" that are laid out in the ghostly grid of what was once the munitions plant.

The road leads to a small graveyard, scattered ruins, and to a campground along an old stagecoach line and the marshy South River.

"Up in our scout's camping area," Hansen said, "some of the scouts and a man who used to fish there a lot said they have had an experience with what's called 'the blue lady.'

"It's described as a blue, glowing apparition that appears with no regularity. The guy who used to fish

34

there in the 1970s was so spooked by what he saw that he never came back!"

The "Blue Lady" walks along the bank of the South River

Across from the old Daniel Estell house, at the intersection of Walkers Forge Road and Route 50, a mound of rocky rubble rises beyond a rickety fence with ancient "No Trespassing" signs dangling from it. It is all that remains of yet another Estell family mansion.

Nearby, where Maple Avenue meets Walkers Forge Road is the Estellville Methodist Church, built in 1834 by John Estell for the families of his glassworks. Acorns are strewn across the sandy soil of the church grounds, and through the graveyard gate are the tombs of several Estell family members and other early settlers.

From that quiet cemetery, Maple Avenue extends into Weymouth Township and, by turning left onto 11th Avenue, into the village of Dorothy.

It was there, in the township municipal building, that Bonnie S. Yearsley, the township clerk, discussed the haunted places of her youth.

The drive along Maple Avenue set the stage for Bonnie's stories. It is quintessential South Jersey. Pines commingle with deciduous trees and rhododendron; numbered streets and avenues are dirt and sand lanes that go nowhere. It is a forest of unfulfilled dreams and shattered realities.

It was the bleak midwinter. Branches of trees reached across the roadway like bony arms and fingers. Ghosts would be comfortable there.

And ghosts, Bonnie assured, were very much a part of the lore of growing up in Weymouth Township.

The land itself has its mysteries. "Weymouth was once everything from the Mullica River south to the Tuckahoe," Bonnie said. "It was a big chunk of land, so vast that the freeholders in Gloucester County didn't really even know what was out here."

It is impossible to ignore the impact the Estell family had on Weymouth Township's history. They maintained several handsome homes, owned much land, and made many ethereal imprints upon it.

One was in the old mansion that is now rubble at Route 50 and Walkers Forge Road.

"The story is that there was a little girl who lived there and drowned in the lake that was on the property. It was her ghost that resided there," Bonnie said as she recalled several adolescent adventures she and many other had there.

"When I was young, the house was still standing and was used as a hunting lodge in hunting season. Most other times, you could get in the house and it was kind of spooky. We would say we'd go there and stay overnight, but we never did because it was so scary."

Bonnie and her coworkers at the township building know about the ins and outs of hauntings. Debra D'Amore, the township tax collector, spoke of a call she received from a vexed resident who asked if there was any record of any unusual deaths in a particular home in the Belcoville area of the township. Although the caller declined to provide details of her experiences, research did reveal that a young boy had died there and previous occupants had had unsettling experiences there.

Sometimes, the possibility of a haunting hits home, as it has for Bonnie Yearsley. "We had always believed that my grandmother's spirit remained in her house after she passed away. And, after we sold it, the people who bought it called to ask about who had lived there because they were experiencing strange happenings there."

Bonnie conceded that the "happenings" might well have been the result of her grandmother's energies. "But," she laughed, " she was a real nice lady, and she wouldn't harm anyone."

☠

The Ghost of Griscom's Mill

There was a mill called Griscom's Mill. A guy got sawed in two down there. That's a fact.

And, there was a house there; they called it the Pink House, right at the sawmill.

"They claimed the house was haunted. There were lots of stories about it, back when I was a little kid."

Edward Layton had just turned 80 when he spun his yarns about the legends and ghost stories around Corbin City, the town tucked against the Tuckahoe River in the southernmost tip of Atlantic County.

If anyone should know about Corbin City, it would be Edward Layton.

We sat in his house on Cat Paw Road—a house he and his wife built themselves, and a house adorned with mementos of the Laytons' momentous lives—Ed proudly spoke of his link with the very beginnings of Corbin City.

"Corbin City was incorporated as a city on July 1, 1922," he claimed, "and I was born on July 13, 1922. So, I was the first person born in Corbin City!"

Adding even more color to that story was the fact that he was born to Cinderella. "That was my mother's real name," he laughed. "She's the only one up in the graveyard with that name."

But, back to the Pink House, next to the mill where the unfortunate worker was sawn in half.

GHOST STORIES OF ATLANTIC COUNTY

"They said that if you stayed in the house at night, you would hear strange noises and see people come around.

"My uncle and I went down there one time. We were inquisitive, just kids, and we spent the night there. Just before dark, we heard something on the roof," he said, a twinkle gleaming in his eyes. "It was squirrels."

"Now, I don't know what others saw or heard, but I know there were a lot of stories about ghosts there."

There were ghost stories elsewhere in Edward Layton's neck of the woods.

"Over Head of the River, people used to see a light at night. I saw it myself, and I couldn't tell you what it was.

"I saw it at least three or four times at night, just hanging over the road. You'd see it in the distance, but you'd never get to it."

The elusive illumination on Head of River Road was, in Ed's words, "A regular light, like an electric light or something. But, you could never get to it. I couldn't explain it.

"I know that a lot of the old-timers, even back in the horse-and-buggy days, would see that light and nobody could ever prove what it was."

Another spot, at the site of an old hunting club on Weymouth Road, has another bizarre story attached to it.

While working for the New Jersey Division of Fish and Wildlife, Ed heard that a particular stretch of land had, shall we say, interesting origins.

39

"At that hunting club is a strip of woods and there's an open spot maybe 50 feet wide that's nothing but sand," he said.

"They used to claim that the Jersey Devil went down through there. It burned the timber there and it never grew back. Nothing has ever grown there."

Even Ed Layton concedes that there is probably a more scientific and logical explanation for the barren soil.

But, this is Atlantic County, the very birthplace of the Jersey Devil, is it not?

Do ghosts stroll inside the Atlantic County Courthouse?

The Haunted Halls of Justice

No place in Atlantic County has been more associated with ghosts and the unexplained than the very seat of government for the county, the county court house in Mays Landing.

Jo DiStefano Kapus, who toiled for many years as a title searcher in the stately building, is the keeper of the flame of legend and lore for the court house ghost stories, as well as many more in the county. Her

GHOST STORIES OF ATLANTIC COUNTY

writings have appeared in newspapers and magazines throughout the region, and she has been a tireless researcher of the history and mystery of the Atlantic County.

A past president of the Atlantic County Historical Society, Jo was gracious and generous in sharing the stories she has heard for publication in this volume.

The epicenter of her research is the Atlantic County Court House that, many believe, is haunted by at least three spirits.

Although renovated and expanded many times since it was built in 1838, the building retains its stately appearance–and its stubborn apparitions.

"Every once in a while," Jo Kapus said, a woman is heard crying, after hours, in Courtroom 1.

"At night, when the building is supposedly empty, the elevator rings as if someone is riding it up and down. Also after hours, lights go on and off and footsteps are heard in empty courtrooms."

The elements of a classic ghost story include any personal experiences witness have had, stories that have circulated about the haunting, and a baseline that could establish the *raison d'être* for that haunting.

All three of those elements are present in each of the stories in the county court house.

The sobbing spirit of Courtroom 1 has made herself known to many over the years.

One was a former senior court clerk who, with two other employees, was wrapping up the day's work in the courtroom when each one of them heard the distinct sound of crying coming from the back of the room.

42

As all three stopped what they were doing and turned their heads toward the source of the sound, they sat in amazement and horror.

"We saw a long shiny thing, like a person," the clerk was quoted as saying. "But, it didn't have the form—just a long, shining glow in the one side in the back of the room."

The trio dispersed quickly. Each used a different exit from the chamber to see if they could pin down the source of the sobbing and the glowing sliver.

They found no one, nothing.

Jo Kapus found something, however. She found it in the pages of the June 8, 1898 Atlantic *City Daily Evening Union* newspaper.

It was the tragic tale of Japhet Connolly, whose body was found in a shallow grave in the woods near Somers Point. The ten-year-old boy has been reported missing two days prior to the discovery.

"The cruel murderer had strangled his victim," the account said. "He had torn the lad's shirt from his body, converted it into a rope and twisted it around his neck until his life was extinct."

The suspect, right from the time the boy was reported missing, was a 28-year old drifter named William O'Mara, who was spotted with Japhet just before his disappearance.

Evidence quickly linked O'Mara to the crime and he was arrested in Linwood before being taken to Mays Landing for trial.

An enraged citizenry called for his lynching, but justice prevailed. He was found guilty on November 2, 1891 and sentenced to 25 years at hard labor.

Could the sobbing spirit that has haunted the courtroom in which O'Mara's trial took place be that of Mary O'Mara, his mother? Or, could it be Japhet's mother?

Both attended the trial and both were reported as weeping throughout the ordeal. So much spent emotion in such a confined space could well have left an eternal imprint that manifests itself still today.

Dottie Kinsey, director of the Township of Hamilton Historical Society Museum, said there have been reports of other spirit activity in the courthouse.

"They hear a child running in an upstairs hallway," she said, "but there's no child there. There are some officers who told me they wouldn't work there because of the incidents.

"Totally, in a collection," she noted, "it sounds as if there is something there."

That would appear to be an understatement.

Lights have been known to turn on without human aid. A chandelier in a court room has swayed and "jingled," an elevator had gone up and down on its own, doorknobs have rattled, and the sound of voices and footsteps in empty rooms and hallways has been almost commonplace over the years.

Some of these episodes have been explained away as natural or mechanical phenomena, but many defy any rational explanation.

Jo Kapus has uncovered other possible baseline incidents that may have added to the supernatural stew that seems to simmer inside the court house walls.

Perhaps some of the energy is that of Joseph Labriola, who was hanged on September 20, 1907 on the courthouse grounds. A contemporary newspaper account was graphic: "The swish of the weight as Labriola's body bounded and rebounded in the air was easily audible through the open jail windows and the women became terrorized. Some screeched and screamed in terror."

Or, the haunting could be rooted or nourished by the imprint left by the man who shot himself during his sentencing in 1984, or perhaps from the fellow who hanged himself in the bell tower in the 1950s, or from a poor soul who suffered a heart attack and died while he and two accomplices attempted to rob the bookkeeping department safe.

County Clerk Michael J. Garvin has heard all the stories. He is non-committal when asks if he believes any of them.

"Recently, though, I was here for a ceremony in which they wanted us to ring the tower bell. We had to go all the way up into the actual cupola. The thoughts of the ghost went through my mind, because it is kind of eerie up there, it really is."

☠

The Scullville Haunting

From the moment Martha Hartman saw the home along Somers Point-Mays Landing Road near Scullville, she knew the place was just right for her.

She could not have known just how wrong she would be.

Martha is a writer, and thus the words you are about to read are hers. We had heard about her stories and asked to interview her. She went one better and wrote down her remembrances.

She had penned a separate account of her experiences (as Martha Geissinger) in another book, "I Never Believed in Ghosts Until..." (USA Weekend, 1993), but what follows is exclusive to "Ghost Stories of Atlantic County."

Her introduction to the entities that would be her constant companions while she lived in the old farmhouse took place shortly after she moved in.

"One night, while alone in the living room, a cool breeze chilled me. I turned to check the window behind me and took a quick blink. A cloud-like puff raced across the kitchen area. I got up to check but saw nothing more so I attributed it to a new house and thought nothing more of it.

"A few nights later I heard a doorknob turn. I went to the kitchen and the basement handle was turning as if someone was trying to get out of the basement. I first thought it may be the former owner, who would come to retrieve items using the outside entrance and yell in to let me know she was there. I opened the door swiftly only to find nothing.

"About this time, I decided I had a ghost. I remembered hearing that if you made friends with it, you would be safe from harm. I did just that, telling it to stay and share my home, but don't harm my children or me. I then went to bed peacefully.

"Late one night a few weeks later, I woke up only to find a small woman with long dark hair sitting in the corner of my room in a rocking chair.

"The odd part was, I had no rocking chair in my room! I never told anyone about this because they would tell me I was crazy or it was a dream. From time to time, she would again appear and sometimes just stand with me."

Martha said there were endless incidents of items falling from shelves, unexplainable noises, the cry of a baby, the faint sound of music, things disappearing and reappearing, and the almost constant sound of footsteps "as if," Martha said, "someone was roaming the floors."

Several visitors, short-term roommates, and Martha's daughter, Kim, all reported incidents or uneasiness in the house.

"I had a weird feeling about my bedroom," Kim said. I used to make my sister come into my room and sleep there at night."

That, we should add, was when Kim was a teenager and her sister was six or seven years old.

"Yes," Kim added, "I think the house was haunted. I think there was a presence there, definitely–especially in the kitchen."

Martha moved from the house, but, as she said, "not without a final goodbye from my spirit."

"I was living between the house and my new apartment so I left a message with my new apartment phone number on the answering machine at the house. One of my brothers called the house and said a woman answered, was very polite, and said I would be home later.

"Another brother and a friend went to the home the same night and knocked on the door but nobody answered. They looked in the window and said they saw a woman with long dark hair standing in the kitchen doorway. She wouldn't open the door, so they left. Later, they came to my apartment and asked me who was at the house. I looked at them oddly when they described the woman they had seen. The other brother arrived not long after and the first thing he did was ask when I was going back to the house and if my friend was staying there all night. 'What friend?' I asked. Then, he told me about the telephone incident and we all just looked at each other. Who was there? Who was she? I had never described her to anyone."

After Martha put the house up for sale, she received a phone call from a woman who said she had lived there as a child. That caller provided chilling revelations.

"Her grandfather died in the house, and his room was off the kitchen. Her grandmother died there of a heart attack.

"I asked her if her grandmother had a rocking chair in her room and she said yes. I then asked her to describe her grandmother. She told me she was short, with a tiny build, and long dark hair."

The woman added something that truly stunned Martha. "I asked what her grandmother's name was, and she told me it was...Martha!"

Martha (the living) is long gone from the Scullville farmhouse. "But someday," she said, "I'd like to go back to the house, introduce myself, and see if *that* Martha is still home."

☠

From the
Barrens to the Beaches:
Haunted Atlantic County

From the sparkling skyline of Atlantic City to the dark woods of the Wharton Tract; from the Tuckahoe to the Mullica rivers, no terrain of any coastal county in New Jersey is as varied as that of Atlantic County.

And, no county has more legends, folk tales, and ghost stories than this enchanted land. Atlantic County, after all, is the wellspring of one of America's most curious and enduring legends, the Jersey Devil.

"We would go riding offshore looking for the Jersey Devil," said John Polillo. "What is was, though, is we would tell other kids where to go look for the Devil and we would get there a couple hours ahead of them and scare them."

50

GHOST STORIES OF ATLANTIC COUNTY

Polillo, a child of the "Beat Generation," a former rock 'n' roller, and a lifelong resident of Atlantic City, sat at the front desk of the Atlantic City Historical Society and recalled the adventures of his childhood and adolescence.

John's twin brother, Joseph, has portrayed "King Neptune" in the Miss America pageant. Together, the brothers have collected tens of thousands of vintage Atlantic City postcards and have parlayed them into a web site and television program that gives viewers a glimpse into the past.

His long, white hair flowing over his shoulders and framing his piercing blue eyes, Polillo admitted that to this day he does not believe in ghosts, but laments the lack of substantive stories in his beloved city.

"Oh, there were the old places we all called 'haunted houses,'" he said.

"They were just old vacant houses. The ones with the widow's walks and witches' peaks were the spookiest. They were down around Mayor White's property at Harrisburg and the bay."

Polillo and his cronies, however, would venture out of the city for their thrills.

"Out by Mays Landing there was **Humpdy Hollow**," he remembered. "You went one way, then to get back to Somers Point, instead of taking Gravelly Run Road or Mill Road back to Northfield you would, just to freak everybody out, go straight into Humpdy Hollow. It was a big, bad, up-and-down road," he quipped.

"That place freaked everybody out."

51

In addition to the "big, bad" road that challenged car suspensions and teenage imaginations, there was also a "big, bad" bogeyman that could pose more of a danger.

"It was a campfire story," Polillo said. "They said that the **Green Lantern**, or the Green Bug, or the swamp so-and-so was out there–and would getcha!"

Dottie Kinsey, at the Township of Hamilton Historical Society, also remembered the many tales of Humpdy Hollow (the spelling may vary).

As for the being known as the "Green Lantern," she said that word spread that it was the ghost of a watchman who was killed (along with 26 others) in an 1880 train wreck in Mays Landing. Historical and geographical facts cast doubts on the veracity of that assertion, however.

As we skip across the county, however, we find many stories that defy any explanation and remain lodged in the minds of those who have experienced them.

One such individual is Joe Naame, who spoke from his real estate office in Brigantine.

"My uncle, Joseph S. Naame, had built a big stone home at the corner of Raleigh and Atlantic Avenues, right across from the Warwick in **Atlantic City**," he said. "He and my aunt moved into the place."

"My uncle was a very flamboyant type of guy with a little wax moustache. He died in 1960, and I was in high school at the time. My aunt moved into an apartment building and she sold the house. It changed hands many times over the years.

"If you're going to have a haunted house, this was the kind of place you'd want. It was quite a place. He had a library right in the middle of it; a suit of armor, big overstuffed leather chairs, and even a swimming pool in the basement.

"Long after he had died and the place had been sold and resold, people kept reporting seeing the image of a man with a wax moustache. One person said they saw smoke coming up from behind the chair in what was my uncle's library. And, my uncle was quite the cigar smoker!"

There were reports that people had actually seen old Joe Naame in full apparition form, sitting on the edge of the bed. One person even said he heard the spirit angrily order, *"Get out of my bed!"*

Old Joe's nephew continued his story. "Down in the basement, around the perimeter of the pool, he had gun cases with his huge gun collection. He had a lot down there—old one-armed bandits from the turn of the century, and that kind of stuff.

"A number of people who lived there claimed they had been run out of the place by the overpowering spirit of my uncle. Even family members of mine said they got chills in the house and couldn't walk into particular places of the house."

Joe never had any personal experiences in his deceased uncle's house, but that doesn't mean he hasn't felt a presence. It wasn't that of his uncle, but of another dearly departed family member.

"One February day a while ago," he said, "I was driving to church. I got this overwhelming feeling that someone was sitting in the back of the car—so much so that I turned around and looked into the back seat. There was no one there.

"I got to church and I was sitting there when a woman I barely knew grabbed my hand in the middle of the service. It was strange. When I walked out of church, that woman came up to me and asked if I had known why she had grabbed my hand. I told her I didn't have a clue. She told me that my mother was with me in church! Well, I looked at her like she was nuts, but it was confirmation for me."

Joe truly believed that the presence he detected in the back seat of his car was that of his mother. And, it wasn't the first time he felt that she was looking over him.

"So," he continued, "ever since that day in church, I truly believe my mother's spirit is with me everywhere I go. I have never really seen anything, and I don't believe in ghosts...but I know what I felt!"

☠

It is said that Clarence J. Geist became disgruntled when he couldn't get a good tee time at the Atlantic City Country Club. So, in 1913, he built his own golf course and country club on Route 9 in **Galloway Township**. He named it the Seaview Country Club and it has grown to become the **Marriott's Seaview Resort**.

Robert Broskey has been bell captain there for nearly 30 years, and he's seen it all. But, we asked him, has he or anyone else seen any ghosts there?

Not quite, but one mystery remains lodged in his mind since it played out many years ago.

"It was winter, it was snowing, and back then we would lock the front doors at midnight," Broskey recalled. "There was a door bell out there, and one night, actually about one or two in the morning, the night auditor heard the bell ring.

"He walked out, and nobody was there. He came back and after awhile, the bell rang again. He went back to the front door again. Still, nobody out there.

A vintage view of the Seaview Golf Club in Absecon

"But then, he looked and he saw footprints in the snow. He figured somebody was standing out front, or maybe they walked around the side.

So, he looked more closely and followed the footprints in the snow.

"The footprints went out to the center of the lawn and stopped, and then they came back to the door," he said.

Broskey said it was as if the footprints came out of nowhere, and went nowhere.

"That's it," he concluded.

"They went from the door to the center of the lawn and back, but there was nobody there, no footprints out."

☠

The "Battle of Chestnut Neck" is but a footnote in Revolutionary War history, but what happened there in October, 1778 was one cog in a wheel of good fortune that kept the colonial army supplied with the materiel of war and soldiers' survival.

That materiel was secured by the derring-do of the privateers who plied the coast and preyed on enemy ships. British privateers raided colonial vessels, and vice-versa.

Little Egg Harbor, and farther up the winding Mullica River at **Chestnut Neck**, were hotbeds of activity for the privateers. As many as 30 vessels would be at Chestnut Neck, unloading their booty, selling it, and getting underway once more for another raid on another British merchant ship.

Enraged by the successes of the colonial privateers, the British admiralty dispatched nine ships under the command of Capt. Henry Collins to Chestnut Neck to "clean out that nest of Rebel Pirates."

Colonial intelligence warned of the attack, and the stores were removed as the port was fortified with as many men and as much weaponry as the struggling army could muster.

The British first set their sights on the supply depot at Chestnut Neck. There, they found and destroyed a handful of houses on land and ten ships in the harbor. Ironically, the ships the British destroyed were captured vessels owned by British shipping interests.

The British then made their move on an outpost of colonial defenders. Capt. Patrick Ferguson and about 250 Redcoats made their way through Little Egg

The "Battle of Chestnut Neck" monument

Harbor in smallboats under the cloak of darkness. They found and raided the outpost on Mincock (Osborn) Island in what is now the Mystic Island

57

section of Little Egg Harbor, Ocean County. In what has gone down in history as "The Massacre of Little Egg Harbor," British bayonets killed some 50 colonials.

Monuments on both shores of Little Egg Harbor now mark the sites of the skirmishes. And, on the Atlantic County side, at Chestnut Neck, some believe the ghosts of the privateers, sailors, and soldiers still linger.

We ventured to the banks of the Mullica as it snakes into the bay and found silvery-blue water shimmering on the river, licking at ancient pilings that jutted just above the surface. It was a calm day that masked the mayhem that broke out there in 1778.

At the Chestnut Neck Boat Yard, Violet Meyer spoke of the remains of a Revolutionary War-era ship that lie beneath the ripples right off the boat yard docks.

Over the years, there have been reports of ghostly troops that emerge from the forests and marshes that surround the neck.

Probably the best place to catch a glimpse of these phantom ranks would be on the tree-ringed triangular plot just off Route 9.

Within that plot, two monuments pay tributes to the patriots and privateers who risked their own safety in the struggle for freedom.

☠

Not far from Chestnut Neck is Port Republic, and not far from that village is the **Clark Burying Grounds** where, generations of locals believe, at least two spirits dwell.

GHOST STORIES OF ATLANTIC COUNTY

"I have never *seen* any ghosts there," said lifelong resident Ray Brown. "I've felt weird presences there, but many others claim they have seen a Revolutionary War soldier walking down by the water near the graveyard, scooping water into his hat, and picking something up from the ground. As soon as he notices that someone is looking at him, he vanishes."

A state historical sign marks the burying ground and the site of the Clark's Mills Meeting House that once stood there. The oldest burial is Thomas Clark (d. 1752), and some folks in the area believe that his spirit also glides through the graveyard.

"In the same area," Ray Brown added, "there are reports of a lady in a white dress who has been seen there, sort of hovering over the burying ground."

☠

The **Carisbrooke Inn** promotes itself as "One Mile from Atlantic City; One Relaxing World Away!"

Indeed, at its location on S. Little Rock Ave. in **Ventnor**, the only bed and breakfast on the edge of Atlantic City's "downbeach" area is a peaceful place just far enough away and close enough to all the "action" a little farther up the coastline.

Each of the inn's rooms and suites are luxuriously appointed, and the innkeeper goes out of her way to make each guest comfortable.

She is Lori McIntyre, and it is she who converted the ca. 1920 guest house into the inn she named after a former oceanfront grand hotel in Ventnor, N.J., that, in turn, took its name from a castle in the town's namesake resort city of Ventnor, England.

Lori does not fully commit to the notion of a ghost in her B&B, but if Stormy is any indication, something mysterious does dwell inside the inn.

Stormy is Lori's cat–a black cat–and she has often tipped Lori off to otherwise invisible and undetectable events.

"Often at night," Lori said, when there are no guests here, Stormy would be on the bed with me, and all of a sudden she would sit up and look around as if there was something there. Try as I might, I wouldn't see anything."

One time, in the off-season, Lori was snoozing in a second floor bedroom and had the door open so Stormy could wander in and out of the room. The cat was on the bed with Lori but, in a flash, leaped up and ran out of the room. Lori was rudely shaken from her slumber.

"It was very dark," she recalled. "I heard a door banging. I couldn't figure out what she was looking for. I was getting really annoyed that the door kept banging."

She tried every possible explanation, but each failed.

"I looked through the opening of the door into the hallway and it was really dark. There were no lights on. But then, two round lights appeared. I watched them for a while. Then, when I opened the door, the lights went out and the door-banging stopped."

She soon noticed that a linen closet door that she was certain had been closed the night before was open.

"It was as if there was something there that I couldn't see, but that Stormy was aware of," Lori said.

Another incident made Lori wonder if some kind of energy occasionally plays games with her.

"We were on our way out for the holiday season, and we unplugged the lights of the Christmas tree before we left. I was absolutely sure I unplugged it. I even double-checked."

Then, she joked, she even triple-checked, just for good measure.

"Well," she said, "when we came home that night, the tree was plugged in!"

This is the first time Lori has shared her stories with anyone. The cautious innkeeper inside her fears that even the hint of a haunting may send timid tourists fleeing from her B&B.

To allay that fear, we repeat what was written in *Cape May Ghost Stories, Book Three* (Exeter House Books, 2002). It addressed an ironic situation:

It is almost amusing that given the number ghost stories in the incredible assortment of Victorian B&Bs and inns on the tree-shaded and gaslit streets of this magnificent city, there are still those innkeepers who have shied away from allowing their stories of hauntings and the unexplained to be told to the public—even though they will confide, "off the record," that they have had experiences with the unknown in their premises.

This, then, has created an interesting phenomenon.

In the course of researching this, and the first two books of this trilogy, we met about a dozen innkeepers who told us they or their employees or their guests have had brushes with ghosts in their establishments. But, because they thought it would be "bad for

61

business" to have those stories published, they opted to keep the stories to themselves.

What this has created is a sort of "Russian Roulette" for those who come to enjoy the charms of a Cape May B&B.

Is the place haunted? If its story is related in any of these volumes, you know it is. You can read the stories, visit the inns, shops, and restaurants, and perhaps have an encounter of your own.

If it is one of the B&Bs whose owners decided not allow their stories to be published (but admitted to have had sightings, etc. in their places), you may never know.

However, if all conditions are right, you just might!

You may awaken in the middle of the night to find a glowing form hovering over your bed. You may be shaken from a sound slumber by the sound of a creaking closet door or a shadowy figure darting across your bedchamber.

You may catch the fleeting glimpse of someone–or something–making its way slowly down a staircase. Or, you may hear the hollow sound of footsteps just outside your bedroom door.

The next morning, as you gather with the innkeeper for breakfast, you will ask about those visions or those sounds. Then, and only then, they may share their secrets with you.

To that end, it is worth noting that despite the fact that Lori had never told anyone, and especially any guests, about her own or her cat's sensations, some guests have volunteered to her that they had detected a presence–a friendly presence–in the Carisbrooke Inn.

GHOST STORIES OF ATLANTIC COUNTY

☠

The building has been a landmark there for more than 50 years. Some may remember it as the Hofbrau, the Vienna Inn, or the Sherwood Forest. Today, it is the **Omni**, a sprawling restaurant and catering hall along the White Horse Pike in **Cologne.**

There, manager Georgeann Atlas spoke of the many unexplained incidents and almost unbelievable photographs that indicate to her and others that the lovely restaurant is haunted.

For Georgeann, it's a no-brainer. She said she has prescience, is sensitive to the spirit world, and truly believes that ghosts walk among us.

"They all call me the witch," she said, straightfaced. "So does my husband. I'd tell them things that would happen before they would. They'd try to get away with something and out of the clear, blue sky I'd be standing behind them."

Having said that, however, the presence at the Omni baffles her.

"I really have no idea what it is," she continued. "Some say it's 'Inky,' a former owner. But, some things defy any rational explanation."

The usual–lights dimming, going on and off, music fading and returning, radical temperature changes–have all played out there.

There have never been reports of any untoward activity in the main dining room. Most of it seems to center in the south ballroom and its kitchen.

"You'd hear things in there and you really wouldn't know until all of a sudden they started becoming very predominant," Georgeann said of the sights and sounds that seem to be most noticeable after parties or receptions.

Something else that shows up from time to time is a shadowy form or an "orb" or two in a photograph taken during an event at the Omni.

Georgeann displayed several pictures of groups, wedding parties, and candids in which the mysterious figures were easily discernible.

Sometimes, the intruder appears as a dark silhouette lurking behind a group of people.

Sometimes, it is a smudge or bubble that some self-styled "ghost hunters" claim is the photographic manifestation of a ghost.

Whatever causes the odd activities in the building or the anomalies in the pictures remains a mystery.

But, to the mystery-loving manager there, that's just fine.

☠

"It's not earth-shaking. It's not ghostly figures roaming the halls looking for a lost love. But it was scary. And it happened to me."

With those words, Carla De Hoyos boldly characterized a baffling encounter she had in an apartment on Ventnor Avenue in **Ventnor**. We will not reveal the exact address.

"I'd like to start on the day my husband and I moved in," she said. "The story didn't happen until much later, but I need to set the scene.

"When we moved in, we noticed a few very odd things.

"The last tenant had left several things there and it looked like they had been in a big hurry to get out."

That, and other perplexing signs in the apartment led Carla to believe that those who lived there before made a hasty exit, for whatever reason. "Also we noticed that in the bedroom," she added, "there were indentations where the previous bed was, its headboard up against the radiator. I commented to my husband, why would anyone do that? It would make the room that much smaller to position the bed that way."

She continued her story.

"I can't remember the exact date," she said, "but it was in November of 1995. "I remember doing laundry and standing in front of my dresser putting away clothes, looking in the mirror. And then, I heard it.

"I heard a man's voice calling my name three times in a whisper. My hair stood on end. It was right in my ear! My eyes started to water (they usually do when I hear a weird ghost story or see something really bizarre on television).

"At first, I thought maybe it was the neighbors, so I ran to their door and knocked, but no one was home. By that time, I was crying. So, I called Fred at work. I was crying such gibberish that he told me to calm down and tell him what happened. I told him about the man calling my name. He asked me where I was standing at the time. I told him.

"Then, he told me that a week ago, he was standing in the exact same spot and heard a woman's voice whispering "Freddy" three times *in his ear!* He told me he hadn't told me because he was afraid I would want to move out on the spot and because we worked opposite shifts and I was home along often that I would be scared all the time.

"He had thought at first it was one of his friends, but no one was outside or around at the time.

"I, by the way, stayed outside until it became dark, and then cowered in the kitchen until he got home."

Carla and her husband surmised that the last tenants had positioned their bed in such a way as to avoid having to stand in the spot she and her husband were standing when they heard the whispering in their ears.

"We decided we needed to move," she said. "My husband told our landlord and he seemed very agitated, almost angry. Nothing else happened there, but we still moved to Brigantine and into our own nonhaunted house that next summer."

"I am spooked just telling you about it," Carla added. "And, my eyes still water when I think about it."

☠

The ghost of an unfortunate motorcyclist is said to haunt **Lake Lenape**, according to stories that have circulated for several years in the Mays Landing area.

There are at least two versions of the tale. In one, the biker simply veered off the roadway and into the lake, where he drowned.

Another more grisly account maintains that the chap slammed into a utility pole along the road and the impact was so violent that his head was ripped from his body and was flung into the lake and never found.

In either case, the end result is that on the night of a full moon, the faint roar of a motorcycle can be heard upon the waters of the lake.

☠

It would stand to reason that in the darkest depths of the cedars, swamps, and pines of early Atlantic County some colorful characters would emerge and etch their names into the history books.

One such character was **Joe Mulliner**.

An outlaw and highwayman masquerading as a Tory, Joe Mulliner was described as handsome, swashbuckling, and every bit the rogue.

Mulliner and his band of as many as 100 men would rob stagecoaches, raid taverns, and ravage farms and mills in what was then Gloucester County.

His exploits became legendary, even in his own time. But, as adventurous and, in a skewed way, romantic as they may have seemed, they often turned vile and violent.

Always one step ahead of the law, Mulliner finally met his fate inside an inn near **Pleasant Mills**. Local militiamen were tipped off that the bandit was there, raided the inn, and captured Joe Mulliner. Justice was swift and certain:

A certain Joseph Mulliner of Egg-Harbour was convicted of high treason and is sentenced to be hanged. This fellow had become the terror of that part of the country.

–New Jersey Gazette, August 8, 1781.

On a hillside near the courthouse in Burlington, the sentence was carried out.

His body was turned over to his widow in Sweetwater and lies beneath a simple tombstone that reads:

**GRAVE OF
JOE. MULLINER
HUNG
1781**

GHOST STORIES OF ATLANTIC COUNTY

Does Joe Mulliner's ghost rise from the grave and haunt the enchanted land around Pleasant Mills? There are those who say it does.

☠

Captain Kidd...Blackbeard...in Atlantic County? You be the judge. Although the comings and goings of these legendary pirates are bogged down in the fog of history, stories of their connections to Brigantine Island and the Mullica River have been passed on through generations of citizen storytellers in the area.

Of Captain William Kidd, it is said that the pirate, having grown weary of life on the sea, was preparing for his "retirement" years by burying vast sums of plundered booty in chests deep within the dunes of Brigantine Island.

He had already met and fallen in love with a girl named Amanda, and it was she who convinced him to settle down as a fisherman or farmer in her homeland of New Jersey.

As he ordered his personal "nest egg" planted somewhere near **Little Egg Harbor Inlet**, certain members of Captain Kidd's crew grew suspicious and found their way to New York. There, they informed the authorities as to Kidd's whereabouts and plans. British warships were dispatched to the mouth of the Mullica where they spotted and surrounded the pirate ship. Ever the cunning captain, Kidd mounted full sail and slipped away from what seemed to be certain capture.

By doing so, he left behind his beloved Amanda and untold chests of gold, silver, and jewelry that are, if all of this is to be believed, still buried beneath the Brigantine dunes.

Old tales told by old-timers also link Edward Teach, a.k.a. "Blackbeard" with the mouth of the Mullica.

While there is no stash of treasure associated with "Blackbeard," legend has it that among his secret hiding places were the meadows and islets of the Great Bay and the Mullica River.

One pirate tale that almost certainly has a basis in truth is that of the "mooncussers."

Some called them "wreckers," some called them "beach pirates." The "mooncussers" moniker is derived from the fact that the practitioners of this particular brand of piracy would cuss the moon on brightly-lit evenings because its brilliance meant that they could not carry out their misdeeds.

The wreckers waited until a moonless night, recruited mules or horses or cows and tied a bright lantern to the beasts' necks. Walking steadily up and down the beach, the wrecker served as a nighttime landmark for unwary helmsmen. Believing that what they were seeing toward the shore were the lights of another vessel closer in, the sailors would be tricked into thinking that they could wheel their ship closer to the shore, too.

The wreckers positioned themselves so that any ships snared by this trap would smash into the shoals or be caught awash by the incoming waves and beached.

GHOST STORIES OF ATLANTIC COUNTY

Should a ship suffer such an unfortunate fate at the hands of the trickery, it would be pounced upon by a band of wreckers and pillaged.

It is uncertain whether the subject of an old ghost story from Brigantine Island was a pirate or a simple man of the sea, but the story of "The Old Sea Captain" has circulated for years.

They say he was the master of one of the many great ships that were victims of the fatal waves of the Little Egg Harbor Inlet.

He drowned in a wreck and his body was never found. But, his ghost forever strolls the beaches of the upper reaches of Brigantine.

He is the omen of a maelstrom the likes of that which took his life. He will appear to the unsuspecting as a weathered old man dressed in ragged rain gear, his tangled, soaked hair flapping wildly in the wind.

He will appear as if out of nowhere, serve as the harbinger of a storm, and when that storm rises, he will disappear into it.

☠

From when it was built in 1976 to when it burned in 1987, the Brigantine Castle was renowned as one of the most frightening "haunted attractions" in the nation. Its mere silhouette was enough to strike fear into all who passed by.

Another familiar silhouette on the beach of **Brigantine** has been, since 1926, the Hotel Brigantine.

More recently known as the Brigantine Inn, much has changed at what is now a fine resort. And yet, one thing seems to remain the same there–its reputed haunting.

In the booklet that touted its opening, the setting of the inn was tinged with intrigue. With these words, the hotel's promoters spoke of what they called "the American Riviera:"

"Voices of the sea that murmur and laugh through the days and nights; The glamour of romance on a silver-beach isle where once roved Captain Kidd and his buccaneer band."

Those legends of Brigantine Island having already been addressed in this chapter, it is worth noting the tales that have bounced around the walls of the Brigantine Inn for decades.

"I've heard people say that at certain times at night, the vision of a little girl in old-fashioned clothes could be seen on the upper floors of the inn," a front desk clerk at the inn revealed. "I've heard that from several guests."

There is also a long-standing rumor that a man killed himself at the hotel by jumping from the roof. His ghost is said to remain there, as well.

☠

No "ghost town" of Atlantic County has suffered more misfortune and generated more mystery than **Catawba**.

All of it can be traced to the foul deeds allegedly carried out by an enigmatic individual named Joseph West.

It was his parents, George and Amy West, who moved from Burlington County to a spot along the Great Egg Harbor River and envisioned a town at what is now Catawba. The West mansion was said to be among the most opulent in the region.

GHOST STORIES OF ATLANTIC COUNTY

The year was about 1800. In the next few years, others moved near the West family, a church was built, and a village was taking shape.

George and Amy West became the parents of three boys and for nearly three decades all was well in Catawba, until...

August 24, 1829: James West, 19, died.
September 3, 1829: George West, Jr., 23, died.
September 10, 1829: George West, Esq., 55, died.
September 15, 1829: Amy West, 52, died.

Counting another son, Thomas, who had died in 1829 at the age of 14, the entire West family was wiped out–except for Joseph E. West.

There was no disease known to be rampant there in 1829, and there had been no reports of anyone in the West family being seriously ill.

But, one by one, over the course of three weeks, all but Joseph died as the result of what has been recorded as "mysterious circumstances."

The sole surviving son dutifully went about sealing the graves, securing the mansion, tying up financial affairs, and–vanishing.

There was never an investigation, as there was no law enforcement agency anywhere nearby.

But, there was suspicion, lots of it, that Joseph West had systematically murdered his brothers and parents to gain control of the family fortune.

No matter what, Joseph West disappeared shortly after the death of his mother, never to be seen anywhere near Catawba again.

Or, perhaps that is not true. One of many legends that swirl around Joseph West claims that when he locked up his parents' mansion, he rigged a shotgun to the front door so that if anyone attempt to break and enter they would be blasted.

The story further states that Joseph himself secretly returned to the house several years after his family's demise, forgot all about the trap he had set, and was shot to death by his own devise.

It is not legend that in the tumbled-down Catawba Cemetery lie the remains of every member of the George West family except Joseph.

There is no trace of the mansion today and scant reminders that on that spot so long ago, a village once stood.

Catawba died because the West family died. The villagers were shocked by the wave of death there and believed Joseph was the killer of his own family.

More than that, they feared that Catawba had forever been cursed and would forever be haunted by the ghosts of the West family.

☠

The following story involves a woman—we shall call her Rachel—her grandmother, and her great grandmother.

And, oh yes, it also involves a couple of ghosts in her grandmother's house on Atlantic Avenue in **Ventnor**.

Rachel asked that her actual name not be used because of the sensitivity of her job and the nature of the familial relationships as detailed in the story.

She has a difficult time talking about her experiences still today.

She's a big girl now, all grown up.

73

GHOST STORIES OF ATLANTIC COUNTY

But, childhood memories in her grandmother's house still lurk on the cusp of her consciousness.

"When we were kids," she said, "we were terrified of going into the attic."

She added that the attic was not particularly foreboding and, in fact, was a fairly pleasant room in which her grandmother had bookcases full of good reading material Rachel and her cousins would retrieve.

"But," she continued, "we would never go up alone. There was one part of the attic you could just not go into.

"It was just creepy!"

Perhaps just fueled by the fears of a child, Rachel's reluctance to enter the attic alone may actually have had a more substantive source.

"One time when I was sleeping over there," she said, "in the room that had been my father's bedroom, I got a really cold sensation and just felt really creeped out. I went down the hall to the bathroom and I saw a white mist floating in the hallway and got a terrible cold feeling.

"It was like a shapeless mist. It didn't look like a person or anything. Well, as I watched it, it turned and floated up the attic stairs.

"I was scared out of my wits and I went into my grandmother's room. She told me to not worry about it. It's just the ghost, she told me, and it wouldn't hurt me."

Rachel saw that same misty figure on at least one other occasion. "That mist was cold and evil," she said, "and talking about it still gives me the chills. There is

74

nobody who could ever tell me that it was nothing but a ghost. It was bad...bad...just bad."

But, there was another incident in her grandmother's house that would involve a much more distinct entity and evolve into a much more profound story.

She and her cousin were playing with a ball on the second floor of her grandmother's house and the ball rolled into the room that had been the bedroom of Rachel's great-grandmother. It was a room the children had always avoided.

"Nobody wanted to go in and get the ball," Rachel said. After bandying the matter about, it was decided that they would venture in together.

"We got the ball and we were walking out," Rachel remembered. "I looked over at the bed, and there was my great-grandmother, Lizzie! She was there, on the bed, down to the rosebud shawl that she always wore.

"I just looked and ran out of the room!"

A familiar phenomenon played out in the next few weeks. Rachel had wondered if her cousin had also seen Lizzie and, if so, why she hadn't said anything to her about it.

"Months later," Rachel said, "my cousin and I were talking and we were remembering, of all things, the time the ball rolled into the room."

After a game of mental volleyball, Rachel and her cousin revealed to one another that both, indeed, had seen the clear image of their great-grandmother on the bed.

The sighting of the old woman has another more emotional dimension. Later in life, Rachel learned that her grandmother and her grandmother's mother had a rather rocky relationship that once prompted Rachel's great-grandmother to leave the house in anger and declare that it would be "over her dead body" until she would ever return there again.

Read into that prophecy whatever you may.

Dr. Jonathan Pitney

The Indomitable, Intractable Dr. Pitney

I awoke in the night thinking that I had heard a telephone ring. Upon opening my eyes I was looking toward the fireplace and perceived the figure of a man dressed in a dark brown or black and long coat regarding me.
When I focused on the apparition, all I could see was the mantel, the fireplace, and the picture hanging over the mantel.

77

GHOST STORIES OF ATLANTIC COUNTY

I felt no fear or shock or surprise, but the image seemed so real for those fleeting moments.

The words seem to be from the pages of a Dickens or Poe story. They are not. Beneath them was the signature of a gentleman who was a guest at one of the most handsome and historic homes in Atlantic County, the Dr. Jonathan Pitney House in Absecon.

Dr. Pitney needs no introduction to anyone who is familiar with the history of Atlantic County and Atlantic City.

Simply said, he was the founding father of Atlantic City.

An 1895 Atlantic City newspaper account said of Dr. Pitney, "If it had not been for this man's energy, for his endowment with an pluck in adversity, who can say that this city would not still be all but a barren waste of sand hills."

Dr. Pitney was among those who carved Atlantic County out of Gloucester County in 1837. He brought the railroad onto Absecon Island in 1854. He lobbied successfully for the erection of a lighthouse at "Graveyard Inlet," the site of innumerable shipwrecks off the northern tip of the island. Oh yes, he was also a practicing physician.

He left his mark on local history, and, many people believe, on the home in which he resided from 1833 until his death in 1869.

"The first time I ever walked into this house," said Vonnie Clark, "I felt his presence. I've never seen him, but once in a while I'll feel that something is there and I'll turn and look, but never really see him."

Vonnie and her business partner Don Kelly bought the 57 N. Shore Rd. property in 1995 and pumped nearly two million dollars into its restoration and opening as a Bed & Breakfast inn.

Ms. Clark is not the only person to sense the presence of Dr. Pitney.

"We had a woman who stayed here, in the Caroline Room, which was Dr. Pitney's bedroom," she said. "She came down and asked if we had a picture of him. She told me that she was in bed reading and she felt a little tired and maybe what she was about to tell me was all in her mind."

Vonnie Clark thought not.

"She told me that the shades were pulled down, but she saw the vision of two men. One was Jonathan, the other was that of a man who was bald and had mutton-chop sideburns. She said she saw them a couple of times."

Another guest who had stayed in the Victoria Room reported a glowing light that seemed to come out of an antique bureau and increase in size until it quickly faded away.

"Whatever that was," offered Vonnie, "the guest said it was as if it was checking the room out. She said she froze as she witnessed it. Before she could get her composure and figure things out, it went back into the dresser." Assessing the situation, Vonnie concluded that it could not have been a reflection or light from the street or the parking lot.

When Vonnie purchased the house with Dan, she had no idea who Dr. Jonathan Pitney was. She is a native of Pleasantville, and thus heard the man's name as it related to the history of the region, but didn't know the full impact he had on that history.

She knows now.

"I had knee surgery and stayed in the Philadelphia Suite for two weeks," she continued. "I asked my daughter to go to my room and get a special pillow for me. I told her exactly where it was.

"She went to the room and could not find it. She spent a lot of time looking for it. I sent her back again and the pillow was lying in the middle of my bed. She said she knew that Jonathan had put it there for me."

Vonnie's daughter, several guests, and even respected psychics have had brushes with the good doctor.

"The psychic, her husband, a friend, my daughter, and I were sitting at the kitchen table having muffins and tea and discussing her walk through the house when a voice came over the speakers. I had a tape of music on and there were no airwaves to have picked up the voice. We all looked at each other and were not sure what the voice had said. The psychic's husband is not altogether a believer, but he did understand the man's voice saying, 'Thank you for coming.'"

Another time, Vonnie's daughter, Michele, was helping her clean the house. "I was singing along with the radio," Michele said. "As I was walking through the kitchen, it sounded as if someone had turned the dial. The station got fuzzy, and then a voice came over the radio. It said 'Stop doing that!' Then, the station cleared up and went back to the music. It was spooky. I said that I'd better stop singing along to the radio—Jonathan doesn't like it!"

Vonnie swore that the incidents were not contrived.

"Many people probably think this is all in my imagination," she lamented. "But too many others have had encounters for it to be imaginary."

The psychic was only a visitor to the inn. Vonnie would never allow séances, "readings", or investigations. She did not want to disturb what she believed was a positive energy in the old house.

She firmly believes it is Dr. Pitney spirit that remains there. Furthermore, it seems to be more caretaking than cantankerous.

On one occasion, Vonnie was carrying a large basket full of laundry down the main staircase of the inn when she lost her balance and started to tumble down the 20 steps.

"I felt as if someone held me all the way down," she said. "It was as if I was gliding down. I got up and walked away." She believed that her fall was broken by the energy of Dr. Pitney.

The fellow whose words opened this chapter was convinced that an entity dwells inside the elegant B&B. His vision took place in the Victoria Room. After he witnessed it, his wife came down and told Vonnie that her husband, a scientist, was embarrassed to admit that he had witnessed a visitation by Dr. Pitney.

Finally, after some friendly coercion by Vonnie, he elaborated. He left his legacy in the pages of the guest register in the Victoria Room.

One couple was not as tolerant of the spirit activity they experienced in the Caroline Room–in which Dr. Pitney died in 1869.

They were high rollers who were placed at the Pitney House by an Atlantic City casino. They opted to leave before their overnight stay was completed. The

The Victoria Room

husband was intrigued by his wife's declaration that the room harbored a spirit and wanted to stay. Nevertheless, he acquiesced after the woman told him that she truly believed the spirit might follow her home.

Was Vonnie upset about losing the guests to the ghost?

"No, not at all," she shrugged. "I told her that if she would stay here and the spirit would really go home with her, I'd rather not have her stay here and take my ghost away!"

☠

The Dr. Jonathan Pitney House

Lake Meone, Smithville

The Legend of Lake Meone

Do the spirits of a doomed Indian couple glide forever on the ripples of Lake Meone?

"The story goes that an Indian princess whose father was the chief of the Lenni-Lenapes in this area was about to be married off to a Seneca chief so he would not wage war against them.

"She had a boyfriend, but he was away when the marriage to the chief was arranged. He returned and found out what her father had done. He truly felt that marriage or no marriage, the Seneca chief would still go to war against the Lenapes.

"The brave and the princess ran away together. And, of course, they were chased.

84

"They reached a cliff at a waterfall and leaped. Both of them died.

"The story now is that on a nice, moonlit night, you can see the ghosts of the two lovers glowing over Lake Meone."

The story was told by Carolyn Handler, just across the way from Lake Meone at Carolyn's workplace, the Historic Smithville Inn.

She spoke with pride of many area legends–of pirates and Indians and, of course, the Jersey Devil. She also recalled another tale that has been told and retold over the generations–the Legend of Quail Hill.

As is Lake Meone, Quail Hill is now within the bounds of the charming Towne of Historic Smithville, a quaint village of shops and restaurants along Route 9.

According to Ms. Handler Quail Hill was named after another Lenni-Lenape maiden transformed into a quail as a means of escape during a raid by the Senecas, who had attempted to kidnap her.

"She prayed that she would escape," Carolyn said, "and she did.

"And when the Senecas looked back for her, there was only a quail on the ground.

"When the Senecas departed, she transformed back into an Indian maiden."

Or so the stories go.

Both legends gained widespread attention with the 1965 publication of "Tales of Historic Smithville Inn" by William McMahon.

In his accounts, the princess whose marriage was arranged to avoid war was named Meone. Her father was Sangreal. Meone's boyfriend was Cabola.

The notion of a "cliff" and "waterfall" in Atlantic County was tempered in McMahon's version of the story in which the couple perished as their canoe was washed uncontrollably from the Mullica River into the breakers of the bay.

As for the young maiden who escaped kidnapping by turning into a quail, McMahon called her Brown Wing, and her transformation and salvation was described vividly: "As the Senecas attempted to drag her away, Brown Wing fell to her knees and implored protection from the Great Manitou. As if in answer to her plea, a sudden wind swept in from the sea, there was a clap of thunder and a tall pine was split from top to root by a bolt from the sky.

"Terrified, the upland Senecas backed away. A torrent of rain descended. When the intruders looked again for their victim they could see nothing but a brown quail who, spreading her wings, flew upward above the tallest trees."

The Senecas fled in fear, McMahon said, and when the raiders were gone and the storm subsided, Brown Wing was found in her lodge "weeping, but unharmed."

Or so the stories go.

☠

The Historic Smithville Inn

The Shipwreck Spirits
of Smithville

The Historic Smithville Inn stands at a most curious crossroads of history and mystery. And, that is meant both figuratively and literally.

Just down Moss Mill Road, and just before that road angles toward Oyster Creek, is the traditional birthplace of the Jersey Devil.

Just across the street from the inn is the Emmaus Methodist Church and its burial ground.

That graveyard may be the baseline for some very odd happenings in the Smithville Inn over the years.

The pivotal event was the April 18, 1854 wreck of the 200-foot wooden schooner "Powhatan."

Nearing the end of its voyage from Rotterdam, the ship carried 29 crewmembers and more than 300 passengers, mostly wealthy German nationals seeking a new life in the New World.

As the Powhatan neared the American coast, strong gales began to brew into a late season blizzard at sea.

The ship was battened down for the worst, but even the dourest doomsayer could not have predicted the ultimate fate of the ship that grim and grisly Sunday.

As the passengers huddled in their cabins and staterooms, warily riding out the maelstrom, the helmsman struggled valiantly against fate to stabilize the vessel.

In an instant, the Powhatan was punched by the wind and smashed into the shoals off Long Beach Island. The raging surf pounded and battered the hapless wreck, tearing it apart with every surge. Passengers and crew scrambled to save themselves, but the situation was hopeless.

Bodies littered the surf and beach for miles in a morbid scene. The storm, one of the most barbarous in the recorded history of the New Jersey shore, claimed all 340 on board.

As the corpses were recovered, they were buried in the nearest cemeteries.

A trench was dug at what is now the Emmaus Methodist Church in Smithville, and 54 Powhatan victims were interred in a common grave in the "Friends Cemetery" section of the church graveyard.

Today, the almost forgotten portion of the cemetery looms in a hollow across from a busy pharmacy and catty-corner from the Smithville Inn.

GHOST STORIES OF ATLANTIC COUNTY

The graves, some just weathered marble and granite stumps, and some embedded awkwardly in the sandy soil, include not only the shipwreck victims but the remains of the region's earliest and most prominent families–Leeds, Higbee, Smith, et al.

It has been said that the cemetery itself is haunted, and the energies that swirl from that haunting have found their way into the rooms of the Smithville Inn.

"When they attempted to bury the victims," Tony Coppola said, "the ground was frozen. So, their bodies were stored in the icehouse in Smithville until spring.

"And, when they finally could bury them, four of the bodies had disappeared. They say that the ghosts of those four shipwreck victims walk the streets of Smithville still today."

Tony Coppola is the co-owner of the Historic Smithville Inn, and he fully acknowledges that the inn and the village that extends beyond it have had their share of ghostly occurrences.

There has been an inn on that site since James Baremore built a one-room tavern in 1787. The present inn took its general configuration in 1951 when Fred and Ethel Noyes restored it and created the village of Historic Smithville. Most of the buildings that house the shops and restaurants were dismantled in other parts of the region and reconstructed on the property. The "towne" became a National Historic Site in 1964.

Although Tony Coppola, his wife Fran and partners Laura and Chuck Bushar have made spectacular improvements to the village, they have not overlooked nor ignored certain eerie events that continue to play out there.

"There have been some strange things that have happened," Tony said. "We took over the inn in 1997 and right after we opened, our alarm went off. I was called by police and I came over. Two police officers were walking around outside and they said everything seemed fine. We went inside and I turned the alarm off. I checked the inside of the building and we couldn't find anything.

"One of the officers left and the other and I went over and we re-set the alarm. As we were walking out, we heard someone walking around in the back room. We definitely heard footsteps. I said to the officer, ' I thought your partner left.' He told me he did!

"We went to the back room, and there was no one there."

Both Tony and the police officer agreed they heard footsteps, and both confirmed they found nothing when they went into the back room.

Tony believed it was the resident spirit's way of greeting the new innkeepers.

Several years ago, Michele Carty worked at the Smithville Inn as a bartender, and she also believed there was spirit activity there.

Michele was introduced to that possibility by a psychic who did reading there on a regular basis. On a slow night, the psychic asked if she could "read" Michele. She declined. "Not that I was skeptical of it altogether," Michele said, "but I was just skeptical of *her*."

But, the woman quickly changed Michele's mind. "She told me how my grandmother used to work there—which I never told her—and that she was watching me whenever I was there. That sort of made me feel a bit uncomfortable."

Michele's discomfort was rooted in earlier experiences.

"I used to have to go down to get the liquor, which was kept under the building. It looked as if it was in tunnels that were under the building. It even looked as if the tunnels went under the street. They were used for storage.

"Every time I went down there," she continued, "it just felt that there were other people down there, or as if someone was watching me. I just felt very uncomfortable when I was down there. The hair on my arms would even stand on end."

The psychic confirmed for Michele that there was someone down there whenever she went into the catacomb-like subterranean chambers–the spirit of her grandmother.

Local legend has it that the tunnels actually led from the inn to the marshlands and could have even been a part of the Underground Railroad through which escaped slaves were shuttled to freedom.

A Smithville shop owner who asked that we not use her name or the shop's name ("I don't want to scare away customers," she said) is convinced that ghostly energies have made themselves known in and in front of the shop.

"Weird things happen," she said. "It'll be real quiet here and all of a sudden the adding machine will whir and buzz and paper will advance out of it. Or, I would hear someone whispering, as if it was just over my shoulder. Sometimes I even picked out a word or two."

The woman said that on one occasion she heard a female voice whispering "Gentle...be gentle..."

"I think that's what she said," the shop owner continued. "It was not what I would call a pleasant voice. It was not what I would call a pleasant experience."

Although the woman heard that voice but once, she feels she may have witnessed a full apparition at another time.

"This is where it gets really weird," she said. "I was helping a customer and concentrating on a fairly big transaction when, out of the corner of my eye I saw the side door open. It creaked and a puff of air came in, and it was quite obvious, to me. Again, I was concentrating on the customer at that moment, but then I saw what I can only describe as a 'filmy' figure sort of glide through the door.

"At that point, I turned and fixed my attention to the form. It appeared to be a young woman, but I saw no real features.

"Now, I knew what I saw, and I knew that the door had made some noise and the figure was visible, if only barely. I know, too, that the customer saw that I was distracted for a little bit. Well, either the customer chose not to respond or didn't even see or hear anything, but neither she nor her friend even glanced toward the side door.

"But, I know what I saw. And, in the maybe ten seconds that the whole thing took, the figure vanished and the door closed."

What did the shopkeeper make of all of this?

"Call me odd, but I believe that there is the ghost of a young woman that seems to be centered in this shop," she said. "I have no idea who she was, why she's here, but to be honest, although the sounds, and that voice and that one sighting did catch me off guard, I sort of wish she would make herself better known somehow."

The Abbott House, Mays Landing

Hosting the Ghosts of Mays Landing

A s we discovered in an earlier chapter and shall learn in the next, ghost towns abound in Atlantic County. There is one "ghost town" (note the quotation marks) in the county that is very much alive.

It is the very county seat itself, Mays Landing.

"The ghost walk is set up to expose our history to more people," said Dottie Kinsey, curator of the Township of Hamilton Historical Society Museum.

She referred to "Ghost Host," an annual Halloween-season event in which the town opens its closet and lets its skeletons run freely as residents and merchants tell the tales of their horrors and hauntings.

The walking tour is equal parts education and

entertainment. As it is a "ghost tour," the emphasis is on the eerie, with a dash of whimsy and a bit of history tossed into the mix.

In its first few years, the walk has grown in popularity and has attracted more and more folks from out of town who dare to stroll the haunted streets of Mays Landing.

"The walk is up Main Street and back," Dottie said. "We ask people in town to share their ghost stories, and we ask them to not embellish them."

Some need not embellish their stories one iota.

Take, for example, the spectacular Victorian mansion at 6056 Main Street in Mays Landing, the Abbott House.

Built in the 1860s by Joseph and Adeline Abbott, the home is a "gingerbread" delight.

It is now a four-room bed and breakfast with every amenity a fine inn can provide. Including, of course, a ghost.

And, if the skeletons of Mays Landing's sometimes colorful past come trotting out on "Ghost Host" night, the eternal tenant of the Abbott House is quite content on staying within his.

He has been called "The Boy in the Closet," and he has drawn the attention of ghost hunters for many miles around.

"I have never seen anything, ever," said Linda Maslanko, the innkeeper of the Abbott House.

"I wish I could tell you something about our ghost, but I haven't had any personal experiences."

Linda did confirm that several guests have felt and even claimed to have seen a presence in the inn, and she admits that her dog has acted a bit strange from time to time.

She does not discount the haunting, but cannot personally confirm it.

Some say they are convinced there is "activity" in the mansion.

The South Jersey Ghost Research organization was allowed to photograph and "read" the building with its technical apparatus, and its members detected temperature and magnetic anomalies there.

And, at least one psychic, who had never been to the B&B before and was not predisposed to its stories, said there was the spirit of a young boy there, and he was in a state of confinement.

Unbeknownst to that psychic, that is the exact story that has been circulating about the Abbott House for years.

The ghost has been identified variously as Martin or David, but has almost always been relegated to the third floor, or attic, according to Linda Maslanko.

"I'm not sure exactly where, though," she added.

It is said that the ghost is that of a teenage boy whose punishment, when alive, was to be locked in the closet. The spirit is most likely to make itself known by opening or closing doors, and is seen most easily by children or teens.

The boy's ghost causes no damage, is of no harm, and seems only to call out to those who can sense it and make them aware of his eternal punishment.

A neighbor on Main Street said there is even a picture of what could be the phantom teenager of the Abbott House.

Michele Dawson said her mother once took a picture of her children standing on the front porch of the Abbott House ("It's my mother's favorite house," Michele said) and, when the picture was processed, a shadowy image of a young person appeared in a second floor window, waving back at her!

That would not be upsetting at all to Michele, as her home is also on the haunted walking tour route.

It is the Dr. McFarland House, 6034 Main Street. Named after a physician who lived and practiced medicine there, it is within the bounds of the historic district. And, it is haunted.

It is haunted not by one, but by at least two spirits that dart in and out of eyesight, stopping only occasionally for Michele Dawson to have a closer look.

"I have seen shadows," she began, "and one time I saw an image in the corner of my eye. I was startled, and as I looked over, nothing was there."

But, she is convinced that something *is* there. She has sensed a "force" near the top of the staircase. She has heard disembodied footsteps. She has had the bathroom door lock flip over on its own and lock itself. What's more, she has seen a full-blown apparition.

"I saw a man standing by the back window," she said. "He was looking out toward the river. I saw it clearly enough to tell you that it was wearing some sort of a suit and a hat, and it was male."

The energies that swirl in Michele's house do so on both the first and second floors. "On the first floor," she said, "I see only a shadow that passes by. Others have seen that, too."

Michele said she is quite comfortable with her incorporeal companions. She grew up in a house in Egg Harbor Township in which the ghost of a little girl was heard and seen, and she has no concern whatsoever that the entities in the Dr. McFarland house may cause concern.

"I had people who wanted to have a séance in the house," she said. "But I told them no. I know the spirits are here, and that's fine with me. I'd rather not do anything that might disrupt anything. They're not malicious, they're totally harmless."

At 6044 Main Street is the Shea House, which oddly enough was named after the Shea sisters who lived there for many years and is now occupied by another Shea family that is unrelated to the sisters.

The present occupants have heard loud noises coming from the attic, "...as if someone was dragging a heavy piece of furniture," according to Christine Shea.

She also has caught fleeting glimpses of something brushing past her, has felt marked and rapid changes in the temperature, and has listened as one of her children described the ghost he saw in one of the bedrooms. "She's a nice ghost," her son assured her.

As a retired registered nurse, the founder of the township historical society, librarian, and curator, Dottie Kinsey might be the last person one may think of as being at all interested in the supernatural. But, think again. She shares her circa 1840s home with a specter she has come to call "The Captain."

Whenever a door would unlatch, or something else untoward would occur in her home, she would blame it on "The Captain."

On one occasion, she may have involuntarily established a line of communication with the ghost.

"My husband was watching a show about ghosts on television and the woman on the show was talking about how her ghost would knock loaves of bread off the kitchen counter.

"While he was watching it, I quipped that 'The Captain' should give that a try.

"Well, a couple of days later, we found a loaf of bread on the floor!"

The sound of footsteps from an empty upstairs room is fairly commonplace in ghost stories. Dottie has heard that sound often. Quite distinctly, she and others will hear the sound of hard heels walking on a bare, wooden third floor. The only thing is, the third floor in their house is carpeted!

"My granddaughter was very talkative as a toddler," Dottie said. "She had a very good vocabulary. I would put her to bed with the intercom in her room. We would listen to her talk, as if she was conversing with someone. It was as if she was having a conversation–she would stop talking as if she was listening and then she would give answers, as if someone else was asking a question.

"I would sneak up the steps every time and I would peek in her room and never see a soul."

One time, and only once, her granddaughter did reveal to her that yes, she was having a conversation with someone she described only as "the woman."

"So," reasoned Dottie, "I truly believe she was having a discussion with 'a woman' up there. Several women have died in this house, so it could have been any one of them."

Dottie really does believe that she shares her home with a spirit or two, and has no problem talking about it. "My kids thought it was the grandest thing in the world to have a ghost in the house," she said.

☠

The Kapus Files

The unquestioned chronicler and champion of ghost stories in Atlantic County is Jo DiStefano Kapus.

As this book was being researched, we followed in her footsteps, guided by the master collector of stories of the supernatural and strange. The retired title searcher has had her stories published in the *Current* newspapers and other journals for more than 20 years, and willingly shared her research and findings so that they may be included in this volume.

Jo Kapus has consistently and wisely balanced mystery and history in her stories. She has also found a comfort zone in which her deep religious convictions coexist with the ethereal world of ghosts.

"I believe there is an afterlife," she said. "The body dies, but the spirit lives on. Are ghosts evidence? Maybe even a warning?"

In addition to "breaking" the story of the ghost (or ghosts) in the Atlantic County Courthouse, Jo found tales of haunted places throughout the county.

One was the Absalom Cordery House on Shore Road in Absecon.

Built in 1817, the house was home to wheelwright and blacksmith Absalom Cordery, his wife Elizabeth, and ten children. In addition to his trades, Cordery was a lay minister and served two terms in the New Jersey senate.

It was written that three of the Cordery children died quite young. It was rumored that when the blacksmith shop was dismantled on the property, the remains of three small bodies were discovered.

Could this be the baseline for the alleged haunting of the Cordery House?

In 2002, Jo Kapus interviewed former occupants of the house. They told of doors opening and closing on their own, pictures falling from walls, and a ghostly woman who wandered through the historic home.

Jack Gubbins, who was 11 years old when his parents moved into the Cordery House in 1978, presented the most riveting account.

"I was going into my room," he told Jo Kapus. "My dad was with me and just as he was opening the door I saw this pretty young woman in a flowing dress in my room. She quickly got up and walked right through the wall!

"I was so scared, I prayed a lot she wouldn't return."

Jo's search for the supernatural also took her to the Sunryser Country Store on North Shore Road in Absecon.

There, she spoke with Margery Durdack and her son, Joseph, who operated the store, deli, and restaurant in 1999.

Joseph Durdack recalled a harrowing experience he had in the quaint building.

"I remember it was nighttime, the store was closed, and I was alone," he said.

102

"As soon as I walked into the basement I heard footsteps upstairs going from the back of the store to the front door and then back again. My mom and my sister and I have heard them before, but each time's, it's scary."

Joseph had already come to believe the store was haunted by a male figure, and upon hearing the phantom footsteps, he called out to the ghost.

"Just then," he continued, "I felt a blast of cold air. The light dimmed and then went bright. It did that seven times. Man, I was scared!"

Joseph had been led to believe the resident spirit was a man when a spiritualist visited and, within minutes of walking through the door, proclaimed that a sea captain and a lady in a white dress haunted the place.

"There's no doubt in my mind that there's a ghost here," Joseph added, "but he's a very friendly one."

Jo Kapus, whose stories always include historical backgrounds on afflicted properties, called the Sunryser "part of Atlantic County history."

She added, "That someone's spirit still lingers makes it even more interesting. Maybe someday we'll know who loves it so much and is reluctant to leave."

☠

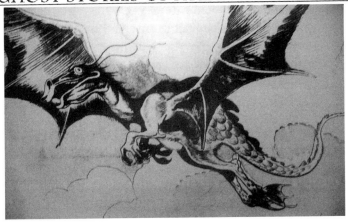

The Jersey Devil

I t is, without a doubt, the most enduring legend in New Jersey, and among the most widely known myths in the United States.

Or, is it not a myth? Did a hideous, horrific beast that came to be known as the Jersey Devil leap from the pines of Atlantic County and terrorize farms and villages for nearly a century?

Northwestern America has its sasquatch, or "bigfoot." Scotland has its Loch Ness Monster. New Jersey has its devil.

So ingrained in the very folkloric fabric of the Garden State is the Devil that municipal governments have included its image in its semi-official seals. Restaurants feature the creature on placemats or wall art. Artists create their own interpretations of the Devil and even scout groups use the Devil's image on patches and at campfire storytelling sessions. The

GHOST STORIES OF ATLANTIC COUNTY

Jersey Devil is a genuine folk hero and a cottage industry.

Several books and songs have been written about him (it?), at least one motion picture was based on the legend, souvenirs are emblazoned with the Devil's image, and the state's National Hockey League team is named the Jersey Devils.

The Ripley's Believe It Or Not! Museum on the Boardwalk in Atlantic City has even mounted the skeleton of the Devil and put it in a prominent place in its ode to the odd. Actually, the museum admits it's a composite made from bones of other beasts.

As we fanned out across Atlantic County researching this book, we learned quickly that our opening line should be amended. Not long after we started our conversations with something like "Hello, we're writing a book about ghosts, hauntings, and legends in Atlantic County. Do you know any?" we learned to add "...*other than the Jersey Devil*" to our spiel.

The guy (thing?) is a household word here.

It's only right. The Jersey Devil is a hometown, uh, hero. He was born in Atlantic County.

We will settle on calling the Devil a "he" because it is generally agreed in the various versions of the story that the Devil was male. What is not as certain are salient facts such as exactly where he was "born," the names of his "parents," and exactly how he could flit about, frightening folks hither and yon and be at both hither and yon at the same time.

Such is the stuff of legends.

GHOST STORIES OF ATLANTIC COUNTY

This is a book about ghost stories. But, to ignore the Jersey Devil folk tale would be folly.

Here, then, is a primer.

We begin as the story began in an 1859 edition of *Atlantic Monthly* magazine:

᠁

...The year was 1735...
...It is well established that one stormy, gusty night when the wind was howling in turret and tree, Mother Leeds gave birth to a son whose father could have been no other than The Prince of Darkness.
No sooner did he see the light that he assumed the form of a fiend with horse's head, the wings of a bat, and a serpent's tail.
The first thought of the newborn Caliban was to fall afoul of his mother, whom he scratched and pommelled soundly, and then flew through the window to the village where he played the mischief generally...

᠁

Mother Leeds, eh?

Was the good woman's name Jane? Was it Deborah? Or Abigail, or perhaps Lucy?

Moreover, was it Leeds at all?

You see, in the tangled web of legend, each of those first names appear as that of the mother of all evil in the pines.

And, Shourds is also mentioned as the Devil's surname, as is an alternate spelling, Shrouds.

Even the very name of the monster himself is different from time to time, place to place. Old-timers

106

in Atlantic County steadfastly called it the Leeds' Devil.

The circumstances that led to the newborn boy becoming a demon are also debated. Depending on the storyteller, he was Mother Leeds' 13th–and thus cursed–son. Others maintain he was the seventh son of a seventh son, and thus doomed.

...little children he devoured, maidens he abused, young men he mauled and battered...

Vague and weak references to Burlington and Pleasantville as the Devil's birthplace aside, it is generally accepted that the beast was born in either Leeds Point or Estellville. The nod usually goes to Leeds Point.

...it was many days before a holy man succeeded in repeating the enchantment of Prospero...the Devil was exorcised, but only for one hundred years...

Given that the birth year referenced at the start of the *Atlantic Monthly* story was 1735, the century-long exorcism of the Devil would have been up in 1835.

Did the Jersey Devil hibernate in a state of suspended damnation until 1835 and then awaken to inflict more pain in the pines?

The magazine account answered that question.

...During an entire century, the memory of that awful monster was preserved, and as 1835 drew nigh, the denizens of the Pines looked tremblingly for his rising...

107

And rise, he did!

Devil sightings were reported numerous times throughout the 19th century, but it was in 1909 when all hell broke loose as the fiend went into a frenzy.

In their perennial regional best-seller *The Jersey Devil*, authors James F. McCloy and Ray Miller, Jr. wrote "Never before or since has his presence been seen and felt by so many" as it was during the third week of January, 1909.

On January 20, he made a brief but memorable visit near his "hometown" as the Devil was reportedly seen–and shot–near Pleasantville.

The Philadelphia Record printed an article that detailed the sighting at Beaver Pond, where telephone linemen were terrorized by a monstrosity that, according to Theodore Hackett, "had the head of a horse, the wings of a bat, and a tail like a rat's, only longer."

Hackett, of Atlantic City, was going about his work on the lines when a coworker first saw the Devil and ran from it in fear. Instinctively, he climbed a telephone pole until he reached the top. There, he panicked and became trapped in the wires. Hackett then noticed the demon, drew his gun, and fired. "One shot," he said, "broke a wing and it fell to the ground, uttering hideous screams; but before anyone could collect his wits the thing was up and off with long strides and a sort of hop, dragging one wing, and then disappearing into the pine thicket."

The grazing fazed the fiend nary a whit. Throughout the remaining days of the week it resumed its rampage and was seen by an estimated 1,000

108

GHOST STORIES OF ATLANTIC COUNTY

individuals. Newspaper reporters and artists had a field day with their descriptions and depictions of the Devil.

As the devil of the pines became the darling of the media in the early 20th century, some folks took full advantage of its perverse attraction.

In 1929, showman Norman Jeffries and animal trainer Jacob Hope hyped the hysteria with a fake letter to a Philadelphia newspaper that claimed the Devil had been spotted in Salem County.

They went as far as staging a "capture" of the Devil and bringing it back from the boonies to the big city, where they put their "living dragon" on display for all to see—at ten cents a pop—at the 9th and Arch Museum in Philadelphia.

Neither dragon nor Devil was this particular "creature." It was actually a rented kangaroo that was painted with green stripes, accented with feathers, and fitted with fake horns and rabbit fur.

Jeffries later admitted the affair was a hoax.

The stunt did not put the legend to rest. In ensuing years, the Jersey Devil was reported in more hithers and more yons and the tale became taller. Word spread that the Jersey Devil was declared the "Official State Demon," but there is no record of that actually happening.

As the wars of the century played out, the Jersey Devil was said to have come to call just prior to the breakout of hostilities. Thus, some believed the beast was a harbinger of war.

If the Jersey Devil is pure legend, if there is not and never was such a freak of nature, what about those thousands of everyday people who reported seeing it?

One explanation that has been offered is that the "Devil" is and was nothing more than an actual creature of nature that stands three to four feet high, has a fearful face, a six-foot wingspan, and shrieks like a banshee.

It is a sandhill crane.

That theory falls apart when certain Devil stories are spiced by accounts of livestock mutilations and descriptions of "a horse's head, a bat's wing, etc., etc."

In her 1986 book, *One Space, Many Places*, Mary Hufford said: "The Jersey Devil legend is not static. It continues to develop, and to vivify life in the region. It has a life of its own. Skepticism is intrinsic to its telling, as it is to every legend."

**...he has frequently been heard howling and
screaming in the forest at night...**

The Energy of Agony

I f the broad brick buildings of the "Atlantic County Facilities at Northfield" seem haunted, it is for good reason.

Spirits do indeed seem to circulate throughout the property, again...for good reason.

The level of human emotion and agony that has played out within the walls of the structures is incalculable. What's more, in the middle of those buildings are the unmarked, untended gravesites of untold, unclaimed bodies.

It is the old Bakersville Burying Ground, the county's potter's field from 1881 to 1955. It is also the epicenter of a vortex of energy that has caused several

111

employees of county facilities to glance over their shoulders, cock their ears, or stand transfixed as a spirit or two coasts in and out of view.

On that parklike vacant land between the Meadowview nursing home and the Stillwater Building (the Freeholders' office complex) also once stood the old J.I.N.S. (Juveniles In Need of Supervision) building, later the C.D. (Civil Defense) building.

Believed to have been the nurses' quarters for the county's TB hospital (now Meadowview), the structure has been demolished, but its ghosts may well live on.

"I always got the impression it was a man and a woman," said Janet Dawson of the inhabitants of the old county building.

Dawson had volunteered there when it was the C.D. Building, and has a storehouse of tales about the ghosts.

"They'd go through the main room and walk through the dining area and back toward the kitchen," she said.

"I have no idea who they were. She wore a gown, like an old-fashioned floor-length gown. He wore a dark suit, with a light shirt. He had a mustache. I liked them."

Well-dressed and dignified, the elderly pair would appear as if from nowhere and disappear around a corner, through a door, or into a wall.

"Her hand was on his arm," Janet remembered. "It was as if they were going to dinner or something."

So often did this phenomenon take place and so emotionally challenging was it that when it was announced that the C.D. Building was to be demolished, Janet Dawson was demoralized.

"I used to talk to them," she confided. "When they said the building was going to be torn down, I asked 'But, where are my ghosts going to go?'"

The strange sounds and sensations were not confined to the main floor and that couple.

On occasion, Dawson said, she and others would hear what sounded like furniture moving in an empty upstairs room.

Or, the sudden aroma of perfume would waft through the air.

Or, a light that would be turned off would turn itself back on immediately.

"There was always something going on in there," Ms. Dawson said. "The things that went on in that building were amazing. Nothing evil, nothing bad, just amazing."

"Often," she continued, "we would be sitting downstairs and it sounded like someone was moving furniture across the floor upstairs, and we all knew there was nobody up there."

The basement of the building may also have been energized. Janet recalled one time when a woman ventured down there to install telephone lines.

"The next thing you know," she said, "she ran up and out of the building. She left her tools and everything in the basement. She swore that she would never come back. They sent two men back to do the work and get her tools."

What caused the first technician to flee in fear? "I don't know," Janet responded, "we never found out."

Perhaps Janet needn't worry where "her" ghosts went. Perhaps they are still there.

Both the Stillwater and Meadowview buildings are reportedly haunted. Various workers in various levels of authority have told of muffled conversations heard in empty rooms, doors opening and closing on their own, and faint images seen in certain areas of both structures.

The incidents at Meadowview have seemingly been confined to the oldest section, the Clyde M. Fish Memorial Wing. Built in the 1940s, that wing was once the "new" county tuberculosis hospital. It was named after Dr. Fish, who was the first resident physician of the earlier TB treatment facility, known popularly then as Pine Rest.

While there may be no connection whatsoever, it is worth noting that the "dignified" gentleman ghost witnessed by Janet Dawson had the demeanor of a doctor, in her estimation.

The Atlantic County Hospital for Mental Diseases, ca. 1909.

GHOST STORIES OF ATLANTIC COUNTY

In the Stillwater Building, several employees–some at very high levels–have privately admitted they have heard, felt, and seen ethereal energies and apparitions in the ca. 1895 landmark.

Activity has been detected throughout the building, and the fact that it served for decades as the Atlantic County Hospital for Mental Diseases may have much to do with that.

Through a certain door, off limits to the public, is an underground oubliette of cramped chambers said to have been the padded cells that once imprisoned certain inmates of the asylum.

Walking within this warren of weird cells conjures up images of those horrid conditions and stirs the spirits that almost certainly dwell there in eternal anguish.

The padding has been stripped from the 8x10 foot cubicles and many of them are now used for storage. Most, however, are empty and eerie.

Pipes and conduits course along the ceiling of the creepy corridor and the doors to the cells have only quarter-sized peepholes through which the keepers could look in and the kept could look out.

One employee said, with the assurance of anonymity, that she is firmly convinced that ghostly energy is trapped there.

"I often see shadows where no shadows should be," she said.

"On one occasion I definitely heard a woman moaning, as if in pain. I can never be sure about this, but I also heard a young man's voice whispering what sounded like the name 'Dan' and the word 'water.'

"I don't know," she concluded, "maybe I was just imagining it all and was just caught up in the creepiness of the place."

Maybe not.

As I walked across the lawn between the Stillwater and Meadowview buildings, the energy level was palpable.

After writing two dozen ghost books, researching hundreds of stories, and experiencing several paranormal encounters, I must say that the old paupers' burying ground holds within it some of the most powerful energy levels I have ever detected.

Not only does the energy saturate that soil, it likely spirals from it to affect and infest the buildings around it.

It is not an evil energy. It is, nonetheless, the energy of agony. It swirls like the steam that rises from a boiling pot.

In Northfield, that pot is the old potter's field of the Bakersville Burying Ground and it bubbles with spirits of the tortured souls whose imprints were left there long ago but simmer still today.

ABOUT THE AUTHOR

Charles J. Adams III is a native of Reading, Pennsylvania, where he resides today.

He is the morning air personality on radio station WEEU/830AM in Reading and is a travel writer at the *Reading Eagle* newspaper there.

Adams has served on-camera and in consulting roles for programs on ghosts and hauntings for the History Channel, Travel Channel, A&E, The Learning Channel, and MTV. Stories taken from his two-dozen ghost stories books have also been reprinted or adapted for use in major publications and motion pictures.

In constant demand as a speaker and storyteller, Adams has been interviewed or lectured in several states, Ireland, and South Africa, and has led ghost tours to England and Scotland.

A member of the board of directors of the Historical Society of Berks County, Pennsylvania for 25 years, Adams has also served as president of the Reading (PA) Public Library.

ACKNOWLEDGMENTS

NEWSPAPERS, BOOKS, ETC.

The Press of Atlantic City, The Current newspapers, The Brigantine Times, Philadelphia Inquirer, *Early History of Atlantic County, N.J.*, Laura Lavinia Thomas Willis and Mrs. L. Dow Balliett, editors; 1915, Kutztown Publishing Co. Kutztown, PA; *A History of Margate City, N.J. for Public School Teachers*, Ralph Robert Levin; *ATLANTIC CITY: 125 Years of Ocean Madness*, Vicki Gold Levi and Lee Eisenberg, 1979, Ten Speed Press, Berkeley, CA; *Longport: A History in Words and Pictures*, Michael L. Cohen, 1987, Longport Historical Society; *Absegami Yesterday*, Jack E. Boucher, 1963, The Atlantic County Historical Society; The Proud American, Josephine DiStefano Kapus, 1982, Standard Publishing Co., Vineland, NJ; *Historic South Jersey Towns*, William McMahon, 1964, Press Publishing Co., Atlantic City; *Pine Barrens Legends, Lore, & Lies*, William McMahon, 1980, Middle Atlantic Press, Wilmington, DE; *Annals of Brigantine*, Paul C. Burgess, 1964, Print-Art Inc., Atlantic City; *One Space, Many Places*, Mary Hufford, 1986, American Folklife Center, Washington, DC; *Atlantic City: Its Early and Modern History*, Alexander B. Irvine, 1868, Wm. C. Harris & Co., Philadelphia;

ORGANIZATIONS

Atlantic County Division of Parks and Recreation, Atlantic County Historical Society, Atlantic City Historical Museum, Pinelands Preservation Alliance, Township of Hamilton Historical Society, Egg Harbor City Historical Society, Linwood Historical Society, Longport Historical Society, County of Atlantic Office of Cultural & Heritage Affairs, Atlantic County Free Public Library, Atlantic County Library System, Margate Public Library, Atlantic City Convention & Visitors Authority, South Jersey Ghost Research, Library of Congress